THE GOLDEN MIRROR

To Ingrid and Marvin:
who have done so
much good with
their service to
our community!

Helmut

The Golden Mirror

18 Short Stories
from a Journey through Life

Helmut Schwab

iUniverse, Inc.
New York   Bloomington

The Golden Mirror
18 Short Stories from a Journey through Life

iUniverse books may be ordered through booksellers or by contacting:

iUniverse
1663 Liberty Drive
Bloomington, IN 47403
www.iuniverse.com
1-800-Authors (1-800-288-4677)

Because of the dynamic nature of the Internet, any Web addresses or links contained in this book may have changed since publication and may no longer be valid.

This is a work of fiction. All of the characters, names, incidents, organizations, and dialogue in these short stories are either the products of the author's imagination or are used fictitiously.

ISBN: 978-0-595-48345-7 (pbk)
ISBN: 978-0-595-71768-2 (cloth)
ISBN: 978-0-595-60435-7 (ebk)

Printed in the United States of America

iUniverse Rev. date 11/21/08

Contents

Introduction

You opened this book; you began to read these words. What can it bring you?

Have you ever driven for half an hour—from home to work or between any two points—and not remembered much of what you saw? Many of us go through most of our lives like that. But many others actually see, perceive, understand, and then share life's joys or sorrows with others. Life can be so touching, so serious, but it can also be so funny and full of joy.

What is our existence in this world? For most of us, it is a struggle for survival in a fragile way of life. Then arise the desires for wealth, importance in society, and entertainment. But does the life given to us not expect mental growth and personality development, the caring for others or public service, also stewardship of nature—and can we not enjoy all the beauty in art, culture, and nature around us?

The following stories are offered to you, the reader, to let you pause and perceive, to touch your human sensitivity and understanding—and also to bring you joy, to simply entertain you.

So, please, proceed! Select titles from the table of contents and begin reading these stories.

When you are done, hopefully you will feel enriched—and, maybe, you will begin to perceive more stories in your own life.

The Golden Mirror

Life can be full of poetry—
the installation of a mirror as a reflection on joy and love

Eva and I had lunch at the small A&B Restaurant on Witherspoon Street in Princeton. Her blond hair looked like a beautiful frame around her face. Her bright eyes reflected the light that came in through the windows. What was she thinking? What did she remember of all the years of our life together? Someone at a table nearby was speaking French, and suddenly, I thought of the French mirror with its wonderful golden frame that we had in our apartment in Cannes.

It must have been more than twenty-five years ago. We were driving through Provence on the way to our newly acquired apartment in Cannes. We stopped for lunch on the central square of the then still quiet, old town of Maussane. All one heard was the clicking of a game of boule, as always played in those places by some local men. A large, old fountain stood there, decorated with funny-looking swans. This was before the town allowed cars to park on the square, which now suffocate everything.

After lunch, we strolled along Main Street—or was it called Rue Napoleon, named for the one who was said to have passed through this town on his victorious return from Italy? We stopped at the Antiquaire, and *there it was that we discovered that grandiose mirror*. It must have been more than eight feet tall. The frame was sumptuous, all gilded in gold leaf. The mirror was surmounted by a wave-like décor, which held a crest showing some convoluted initials. I promptly interpreted the initials as Eva's, "ES"—or did they relate to Eugénie, the most beautiful (and quite daring) daughter of a local nobleman remembered in Romantic poetry? I bought the mirror for our new apartment, and for all the years I was to see Eva reflected in it as *my* Eugénie.

When we hung the mirror on the wall of the Grand Salon of our apartment, Eva lifted up one of our young sons that he could see the mirror a little better. He stretched out his arms in joy. Years of light and happiness began for us in Cannes.

In the mornings, when we woke up, we could see the bright blue morning sky reflected in the mirror. Lifting our heads a little higher, we could see the tall old pine tree outside in the light of the sun, and behind it, the golden beach, the blue expanse of the Mediterranean dotted with white sails, and, in the distance, the Lerins Islands.

Later in the day, we often sat in our garden, surrounded by agapanthus bushes, blooming oleanders, and the palm trees we had planted. Whenever we looked back into the coolness of the apartment, behind its thick stone walls, we could see the mirror. Reflected in it, we could observe whether any of our small children were resting on the bed—for once, in angelic tranquility—or whether they were up to something that we should know about.

Occasionally, I would be the one to rest on the bed. In my dreams, I could sometimes see all the characters of my stories descend from the mirror as if in a procession through a tall golden gate—even the little animals of our garden were somewhere on the side, and a small colorful ball rolled along in front, driven by the wind. What a reflection of our journey through life.

How happy I was when Eva woke me up by looking in from the garden with a smile, calling me to come for a swim!

On cool evenings, we often sat on an uncomfortable, but antique, sofa under the mirror, or on equally uncomfortable antique chairs around the table where we played a French card game called Tarot. It was a running joke with us whether the mirror would let us look into the cards of our opponent.

Time passed. Our children grew up, went to college, and got jobs. There was no time left for long vacations in Cannes—on the beach, in the garden, and in the apartment.

Finally, we sold the apartment, and so the day arrived for us to move away. One of our sons came to help us move the heavy furniture. We had intended to leave the mirror behind, possibly selling it in Cannes. But our son protested, saying that he remembered how happy we had been when we had just obtained that mirror. He thought we should take it with us. He would want it later, he urged, once he had a better job and a suitable apartment of his own.

I rented a small delivery van, one just big enough to hold the furniture we wanted to take along, including the mirror, but a bit too big for comfortable driving.

I admonished Eva, in case she might be driving for a while, to be very careful, "not to cut corners with this kind of vehicle." Those big vehicles could take along anything she got too close to. In the end, we decided that I would drive— 650 miles in one stretch, all the way to our new apartment in Munich. I was dead tired when we arrived late at night.

I spotted the perfect place to park, which happened to be in front of a new-looking Mercedes. I turned in. We heard a crunching noise! I had turned too sharply around the Mercedes and scratched off one of the car's headlights. Eva looked at me for a moment, then said, "You must be very careful not to cut corners with this kind of vehicle."

Our new apartment in Munich turned out to be too small for the big mirror. Its grandiose French frame looked lost among the Nordic, utilitarian Ikea furniture. So we stored it in the basement section allocated to our apartment, tightly wrapped in an old blanket of faded turquoise color and further protected by an old, blue foam rubber camping mattress. What a descent for the noble mirror— no more sun and light and happiness to perceive and reflect for many years to come! Occasionally, when I had to get something from the basement, I could just make out the golden top of the mirror décor with the crest reaching up from its ugly restraint, as if pleading with me for a new life in the sun.

One day, we visited one of our sons, who then lived in San Francisco. He had purchased a beautiful condo apartment in the

Marina district, only a block from the Bay. There was access to the flat roof of the building. From there, we had an enormous, sweeping view of the Golden Gate Bridge, the blue expanse of the Bay dotted with white sails, and, in the distance, some islands.

"It looks a little like the Mediterranean" I said.

"Do you still have the old mirror?" he asked.

A few months later, we found a convenient way to ship the mirror from Munich to San Francisco. On our next trip to see our son, I helped him hang it on the large wall behind his dining room table. Even our son's girlfriend agreed that it looked very beautiful there. As the French would say, "Ça fait Grand Salon."

And when you look from a certain angle, you can see the blue sky and the golden sunlight of California reflected through the living room window. Dreams of Cannes?

We really had to mount the mirror solidly to the wall—on account of possible earthquakes there. When all was done, late in the evening, Eva held up our young granddaughter from another son so she could see the mirror a little better. She smiled and stretched her arms out in joy. Then we played a game of Tarot, sitting together at the dining room table on rather uncomfortable kitchen chairs. Our son said that he could see my cards reflected in the mirror—again.

Before we retired for the evening, I looked once more into the mirror and saw Eva reflected in it as she stood next to me. Her blond hair looked like a golden frame around her face. Her bright eyes reflected the light. Her smile had a bit of Eugénie.

Did she think of all the happy years of our common journey through life?

Hello, Eva! I still love you!

Tiger Joe

*

A failure in life—but always remembered by me

*

One evening in Arizona returns to my thoughts again and again. On that evening, so many years ago, I saw Joe for the first time and the last time. Or did I?

It was October of 1978, in Scottsdale, Arizona. The crowd of summer tourists had departed. The winter visitors had not yet arrived. The days where still sunny and warm, but the evenings became refreshingly cool. My old colleague, George, and I had met at the Grapevine Restaurant. Many went there in those years to see the young waitresses, but we just wanted to sit under the clear night sky on the open terrace on the roof and have the specialty of the house, Greek pizza.

George was close to seventy at that time, and he appeared tired. He talked about his great project. He wanted to write a book—more than that, an analysis and a comprehensive theory, many volumes long—of the whole human society. I suggested that he proceed in small steps, beginning with a short article on one aspect of the subject. I urged him to do it soon, while he still had the energy to think and write. Life passes so quickly.

It became too noisy at the restaurant, so we drove out of town, north, toward a small place beyond the town of Care Free. We soon left the endless suburban developments behind. We passed Raw Hide, the recreated Western town and a movie set for many cowboy films, with hourly shoot-outs every evening. As the road climbed through the darkness to the distant hills, the thousands of lights of Scottsdale were still visible in the lowlands, spread out as if on a jeweler's tray. The sky, with its brilliant stars, extended far above us and the dark desert. A rabbit ran across the road and the beam of the car's headlights, and then took cover behind a cactus.

Soon we approached Care Free and its enormous red boulders. We crossed the town, passed the elegant winter homes of wealthy Northerners, finally reaching the older houses of Cave Creek. Right in front of us was a big building, like a low barn, made of gray, old wooden boards—"Chuck's Corral"—at that time lit only by a single street lantern and a red neon beer advertisement at the door. We decided to stop and go in for a drink.

The hinges of the old door squeaked as we entered. The inside was just as dark as the outside. The large room was furnished with dining tables, but nobody was sitting at them. An old jukebox with typical multi-colored lights stood at the back wall. Along the right wall, at the back, was the long bar. Was that a single bulb hanging from the ceiling to provide some light? Two old men sat at the bar, wearing cowboy jackets and hats, as if they were in a Western movie. The bartender, bald-headed and with a dark mustache, was reading a newspaper. He glanced at us only briefly as we entered.

George and I ordered beer.

After a lengthy silence, I mentioned to one of the old-timers, "It's getting cool outside."

"Yep," was the concise answer.

Silence again.

"It's quiet around here," I said.

After some hesitation, the answer came, "Yep."

Another long silence was broken by the surprising question, "Where are you guys from?"

We had been accepted, and those old-timers at the bar were ready to communicate with us.

Soon we learned that both men were retired and had lived here alone for some time, since both had lost their families. What else did they do up here?

"Not much," they said.

Silence fell again.

Finally, one of them said, glancing at his partner, "Joe has his tigers."

Tigers?

Now, it was my turn to remain silent for a while.

Then I said, "That's good."

"That is *not* good," the man said. "It costs quite a bit to feed them."

After the appropriate time, I agreed, "No, that is not good."

I had swallowed the bait; now came the hook, "For a donation, Joe might show them to you."

They had found a use for us and hoped for some entertainment, it seemed.

The one addressed as "Joe" was short and very thin, with a wrinkled, unshaven face, as if the desert heat had dried him out. He looked at us with dark, tired eyes, as if pleading.

I looked at George, and he looked at me. Silently, we acknowledged to each other that we were in for something. Tigers at Chuck's Corral in Cave Creek— certainly a very safe arrangement in this oversized chicken coop with these guardians. Or were they only paper tigers?

Finally, I pulled out five dollars and put them on the bar next to Joe.

"That much for each of you," said the other old-timer. What a character! He must have been a businessman, in his day, or a horse trader—or he knew a "dude" when he saw one.

It was worth it just to have some fun. I put the second five-dollar bill on the bar.

Joe almost smiled. He finished his beer and got up.

We thought it made sense that we also finish our beers and follow him.

Joe walked to the far end of the bar, to a door on the back wall. It squeaked as much as the front door when Joe stepped outside. We followed.

Outside, the night was as black as ever. Joe disappeared into the darkness. Then, with a click, five lights came on. Mounted on high poles, they provided unexpected brightness. But even that amount of light was meager for the large sand court that we now saw. To the left, an old wrecked car—a Chevy—then a low, rusted corrugated metal shack, and then another wreck—a brown pick-up truck—between some tires and abandoned car parts. Behind the sand court and to the right, we saw huge rock formations, totally enclosing this space.

To our surprise, a circular chain-link fence occupied the center of the court, less than twenty feet in diameter and about twelve feet tall. A low chain-link tunnel led from the circular fence to the corrugated metal shack. We noticed high stools, like those in a circus, in the circular fence.

Joe looked at us to see whether we believed him now. His buddy looked upon all this with an expression of great pride—it was he who had told us about the tigers. The bartender appeared at the door to watch our reaction.

I said, "Where are the tigers?"

Joe gave me an offended look. Did I still not believe him?

He walked to the back of the shack. I followed him in three big steps.

"Don't scare them!" he said. "They don't like to get up at night."

He opened the door to the shack. An intensive stink emanated … as of tigers!

Inside, Joe turned on a weak light. Behind a grill, I slowly made out four long piles on the floor.

"Hey!" Joe called, "Hey, hey!"

He grabbed a long pole and poked the piles. The head of a tiger came up, then a second.

It took some time, but eventually four tigers were up on their feet.

They *were* tigers. Or were they only tiger skins, loosely hanging from some long bars in folds? Those were certainly the oldest and skinniest tigers ever seen, something for the *Guinness Book of World Records*.

Joe kept poking at the tigers, poking and poking, calling each by its name, until the first one slowly walked over to the opening leading out to the fenced tunnel. And this was real tiger walk—inaudible, elastic, almost flowing, but in slow-motion, resigned, no longer prowling.

The other tigers followed, assessing us furtively as they passed. The last one got an extra poke from Joe and turned around with a deep, threatening growl— an echo of times past, a recall of the life of his ancestors in the wild, of his own youth in the circus arena—like thunder waning in the distance.

We left the shack to observe the progression of the four big cats through the fenced tunnel. Could it be that some green light still glimmered in their eyes? Once inside the ring, each tiger jumped up onto a stool, smoothly and swiftly, in this brief moment showing its enormous size and remaining power. Then, all four of them sat quietly.

Joe entered the ring through a small door and locked it carefully behind him. He had left his hat outside. Now he held a whip and a large hoop in his hands. The show was ready to start.

Joe stood upright now, tense, as if a younger version of himself. His voice was strong, clear, determined. The whip snapped. The tigers cowered. Suddenly, two tigers on opposing sides jumped at the same time, one above, the other below, from their stools to the stool just vacated by the other tiger. The remaining two tigers became nervous. Growling, they showed their paws. One snap of the whip from Joe, one short command, and they, too, jumped and exchanged seats. Joe turned slowly and carefully toward us, not taking his eyes off the tigers. George and I, the only guests, applauded vigorously. But the sound was lost in the large sand court. Only a ghostly echo returned from the rocks, as though from a larger audience of a faded past, no longer living.

"Hey!" Joe called in the ring, "Hey, hey!" He held the hoop up. "No fire any more!" he called over.

"Not permitted here, you know," added his buddy, who was standing next to us. But how did Joe mean that? Joe, you are still what you once were! At this moment, your fire of life is still within you!

One tiger jumped through the hoop, then a second. Then Joe waved them off.

"They're getting tired," he said, throwing a morsel of food to each one. While the tigers gnawed greedily at the tiny chunks, Joe turned to us. With a sweeping motion of his arm, he bowed to indicate the end of the show, then he stood up straight and tall. We applauded again, longer and louder than before.

The tigers moved back through the tunnel. It appeared as if they held their heads a little higher, as if their walk were a little fresher. They hesitated at the opening to the shack. But then the first one glided in, followed by the second one, then the third, and, finally, after a last look back at us, with his head lowered, the last tiger disappeared. I will not forget that last look back of this tiger before he walked into the darkness of the old shack.

Joe remained alone in the ring, holding on to his whip and hoop. He put them down slowly, came out of the ring, and locked the door carefully, seeming to hesitate.

Joe's buddy turned to us. "Very good!" he said with pride in his voice. Joe looked at us insecurely.

"Excellent tigers!" I said.

"Excellent show!" said George … for Joe.

We went back into the bar.

I was still in the doorway when Joe switched off the lights in the court.

Total darkness and silence surrounded us again. Had all this been a dream?

At the bar, I ordered a round of beer for everyone. Joe appeared more lively.

"What do you feed them?" I asked. After all, my $10 was meant for food for the tigers.

"Heads and wings," he answered.

"Whose heads and wings?"

"Chicken."

We learned that Joe obtained any quantity of chicken heads and wings he wanted from a friend at a poultry company. That was what the tigers ate every day—every morning and every evening, sometimes only once a day—nothing else, except when Joe had some money. On such occasions the tigers got real meat—discarded by a meatpacking company. But that company wanted money, even for discarded meat; that's what our $10 was for.

Who else came to see the tigers?

"Many visitors," said Joe.

"Occasionally some school children," said his buddy.

"Not occasionally—all the time!" said Joe. "I will still open my zoo and circus. Soon. Maybe next year."

Joe then talked about his life, his big dream for the future, his plan, his project. The tigers came from a circus that had gone bankrupt just when it had passed through Scottsdale many years ago. The owner had disappeared across the border to Mexico with all the money. The auction for the tent, wagons, and animals did not even bring enough to pay the creditors. Nobody wanted the tigers; they needed too much meat. Joe, the caretaker for the tigers, could not leave them behind. He could not abandon "his" animals. So he took them in and made it his life's work to care for them.

After some wandering around, he found a refuge for his tigers in the court behind an abandoned garage in a side street of Cave Creek behind Chuck's Corral. He had observed enough of the original tiger tamer's work to now put on a modest show himself. The tigers worked with him because they had known him for so many years, and because he had always saved them from starvation.

This had gone on for many years. The plan for the big zoo and circus had also been discussed for many years. Many more animals would be needed for really big shows.

"He always talks about it," interrupted the bartender.

"I'll do it," Joe said. "Next year ... if I have enough money by then."

"He should have done it years ago, when he was younger and had more money," said the bartender.

"I *will* do it," said Joe, "But I need some money first. Maybe more school children will come this year. Maybe I'll ask them to pay a little to see the show."

Now we learned that school children could see the tiger show for free. Occasionally, the children made voluntary donations of some dimes or quarters. Joe used these to get real meat—for his tigers.

And the tigers got old.

* * * *

So many years have passed since.

Last year, I had some business in Arizona, again. Chuck's Corral was still there, had become a fancy restaurant. This time, there were more than just two guests. I learned that Joe had died several years earlier. And his tigers? The Humane Society came and took them away. Only the old chain-link ring still stood in that court in back where nobody went any more.

I telephoned George. He had just turned seventy-eight. His book, his large report, was still in the making. He still hoped to finish the final draft soon.

I am getting older, too. As soon as I find the time, I will start writing a story. I have a great idea: the story of Joe and his tigers! But I should start writing now. Soon. Maybe next year.

When I'm finished with the story, I will step outside one night, when the stars are brilliantly clear in the dark sky above, extending far over the wide open land. I will marvel at the constellations of the stars where ancient people saw fabled animals and recognized the actors of their stories.

Isn't that the constellation called the "Tiger" there?

And what do I see in those stars right next to it?

<u>Joe!</u>

The Raritan River Ferry

*

A discarded ferry—
the story of an old man—
and a child's thought for you

*

I caught myself dreaming one day. About great things. About the great things which I had wanted to do in my life and hadn't done: the remodeling of our house, a trip along the length of the Andes, the writing of a short story, some really significant writing. Why do I never get to do them? Too many little things have to be done first. My budget runs low. My job does not leave me any time. My inertia. Ah, when I retire, then I will do all these great things.

Next morning, I woke up from one of the bad dreams that befall me from time to time. I had seen an old ship anchored behind a red buoy. I had thought how nice it would be to go on a big trip on this ship. Then, I saw workmen come and remove the engine from the old ship. Never would it travel again. I was deeply saddened. Why had it not left before the workmen came? Did the red buoy stop it? What nonsense.

For most of that day, I felt a bit depressed, a bit confused. Late at night, when the clock had just struck midnight, I started to write the story of the ship.

✱ ✱ ✱ ✱

Entering the New Jersey Turnpike at Exit Nine, going north, you immediately cross the Raritan River over a large bridge. Few people notice the river—most are too busy concentrating on merging into the New York-bound traffic. But that is the place where you should look—right, over the bridge railing—toward the river. Choose the truck route on the right side of the turnpike; then you can get an even better view of the river.

The Raritan was once a beautiful river. At New Brunswick, the river leaves the Piedmont between the steep slopes of the last hills, which formed millions of years ago when Europe separated from the North American continent. The main branch of the gray-blue Raritan flows there east through the sedimentary plain toward the Atlantic, gaining in width, winding in gentle curves, and framed by an increasingly broad belt of swamp grasses, tender and green in spring, golden and brown in fall.

In olden days, ships with passengers and cargo came up the river from New York to New Brunswick. From there, passengers and freight continued along the King's Highway, now Route 27, via Princeton to Philadelphia, or further yet, to Baltimore or Washington. Ships no longer come up the Raritan. Railroads, cars, and trucks rumble along tracks and highways connecting north and south. Several bridges cross the river. The newest and largest is the Turnpike Bridge, six lanes in each direction, a total of twelve lanes wide, and all lanes are used intensively. Nobody has the time to look over the railing at the river.

The Raritan at New Brunswick is no longer beautiful. Modern development brought garbage problems. Big cities and industry brought junk. A whole scrapped ferry boat was deposited on the shore of the Raritan, in the midst of the swamp grass, just a few hundred yards east of the Turnpike Bridge. A much smaller boat was deposited next to it and, in front of both, still floating in the water, rests a buoy.

The big ferry once plied the waters of the New York harbor, going back and forth between the city and the towns on other shores. It is a big boat, long and wide, two-storied, and painted in a lively yellow color. At each end, a little hut just big enough for the captain and the helmsman sits on top. Those huts are painted a light blue-gray and are located high up at each end so that the ferry can go back and forth. In the center of the ferry is the big smokestack, painted pink— very pretty. That was a beautiful boat once. Now it rests half-tilted in the swamp, surrounded by the tall reeds. The bow just touches the open water of the Raritan.

The small boat next to it is white. You would not notice it unless you really looked. The buoy in the water also came from New York Harbor. It is painted red, with a small metal tower on top and a square panel mounted to it.

For eighteen years, I had been crossing the bridge. Whenever traffic permitted—on hot summer days, in the snow in winter, on brilliant mornings, on foggy evenings, even in the moonlight—I looked at the ferry. Otherwise, I knew nothing about the ferry.

Until I asked the old toll collector at the Turnpike's Exit Nine, who sat there contentedly as I paid my toll.

"What's the matter with that stranded ferry downriver?" I asked.

"That is quite a story," he said.

"What kind of story?" I asked.

"Requires too much time to tell here," he said, as somebody honked behind me, in a hurry to get through the same tollgate.

Two weeks later, I visited with Henry, the old toll collector, at his tidy, little house. It was in the old part of our town, where the houses stand closely together, on a quiet, narrow side street. There, all houses still have covered wooden porches a few steps up, with comfortable chairs or even an old sofa. Everybody used to sit there on warm evenings—old couples, young people, sometimes the whole family—talking with the neighbors across the street and to the sides.

It was just such a warm summer evening, so we sat on Henry's porch. Right away, Henry's grandchildren, a little girl and boy, came and sat there with big eyes, ready to listen to whatever we had to talk about.

"Grandpa, can you tell us about your trip around the world, again?" asked the little girl.

"Or about some more adventures during the war?" asked the little boy.

Apparently, Henry had traveled quite a bit in his younger years and had experienced many adventures. Now he lived quietly, particularly since his wife had passed away a couple of years earlier. Lately, his own health was declining, so he could not travel anymore.

When the children learned that we would be talking about the ferry, they called their friends from across the street, "Henry is telling the story of the ferry again!" Quickly we had several small children around us.

"Well," said Henry. "Well, well. I will tell you once more what really happened to me many, many years ago.

"In those years, when I was much younger, I liked to fish, especially on the Raritan River below New Brunswick. Now, every fisherman knows that some fish bite best at night, especially when the full moon is high up in the sky.

"It was on one of those beautiful nights in spring when I got into my little fishing boat and let myself drift down the quiet river. The water stood very high. That happens when the full moon produces a high tide, which doesn't let the water leave the river for the ocean. I had a fishing line hanging down from each side of my boat. The moon looked so beautiful in the sky. It gave a soft light to the scene. I was so happy. I felt as if I were part of nature. There were the voices of the night animals here and there, of frogs and unusual birds ... but that—what was that?

"'Krrrrrrrrr ... queeeeeeek ... krrrrrrrrr ... queeeeeeeek,' on and on.

"I quickly pulled the fishing lines in and laid down as low as I could in my boat, always listening to that noise. The further along the river I drifted, the louder it seemed.

"'Krrrrrrrrr ... queeeeeeek ... krrrrrrrrr ... queeeeeeeek.'

"Now I could hear some other sounds.

"'Krrrrrrr ... tock tock ... queeek ... click click ... krrrrrr.'

"Slowly, my boat moved closer, drifting to the side of the river where the high reeds stand. As it moved around a bend of the river, I suddenly saw a large boat in the moonlight in front of me. It was painted yellow. High on top, at each end, were the small captain's cabins, painted blue-gray. The smokestack, in the middle of the boat, was a light rose pink."

"Oh, how beautiful!" said Henry's granddaughter.

"Don't interrupt all the time!" said her brother.

Henry continued, "The big boat was wedged sideways between the reeds, but the bow stretched out into the open water of the river.

Since the water ran high this night, it may have lifted the boat, moving it lightly with the movement of the water. Was that all? I didn't trust those noises. Stretching my hands over the sides of my little boat, I paddled as quietly as I could toward the reeds. Then I pulled myself by reed stems deeper into the thicket. Nobody could see me there. But I could observe the big boat through the last row of reeds.

"I heard a distant clock strike twelve times—midnight. Not far from me, an owl called out with a sad cry. Then I heard a big yawn, very close, from the direction of the boats.

"I sat motionless in my own small boat, pressing myself real low, eyes wide open, and my ears—I wished I could have made them larger!" and Henry pressed himself so deep into his chair that he could just barely look out over the banister of the porch to the dark street beyond. It was very quiet. The children all sat there, motionless.

"Then I heard a small yawn, 'haaawwwwww!'" continued Henry after a few moments to let the suspense build up.

"I saw a smaller white boat—a runabout—next to the big boat, also moored between the reeds. And in front of them in the water … what strange thing was that?"

"The red ghost!" said Henry's grandson.

"Yes, really." said Henry. "It was a small red ghost. It was balancing on a red buoy, swaying back and forth. It kept its arms tightly to its sides and had a big, square head. Only as my shock wore off did I realize that it was a red buoy with a small tower mounted on top, swaying with the waves of the river. But what was happening now?

"Shutters opened on each side of the ferry. Two windows were illuminated by a weak light, as if the big boat had eyes. The same happened on the small white boat. Two headlights turned on, looking like two bright little eyes. And on the head of the buoy—were those two big fireflies with their greenish light?

"I heard the voice of the small white boat, 'Did you wake up, big ferry?'

"'Oh yes,' answered the deep voice of the ferry, as if coming out of the depth of a big metal barrel. 'Did midnight at full moon come up again?'

"'You must continue the story of the big storm of 1921, which you couldn't finish last time!'

"'Oh, yes! That was a real bad one!' said the ferry, wide-awake now. 'The night had come, and the weather was worse than ever before. The storm blew so wildly that the whole harbor of New York churned as if it were the high seas. Just as I crossed the middle of the harbor to return to the city, a big ship full of people came by. And then it was blown over by the storm. Everybody was thrown into the water. I shifted my engines to the highest speed, turned my big siren on, and fearlessly, I hurried right into the mighty storm toward the capsized ship. I saved the people. All of them! I stayed in the storm until everybody was on board. Then I quickly turned around to the city, to let the people get dry and warmed up again.

"'Next day, the mayor of New York came and brought a flag of honor. I flew that flag for a whole month while going back and forth across the harbor. All other ships were ordered to make room for me.

"'Another time, the King of Sweden visited New York. He was scheduled to cruise the harbor aboard a nice, white yacht. But when he saw me, he thought I was more beautiful and wanted to cruise with me. A band came aboard and played music while I cruised with the king on that sunny day to the Statue of Liberty on its little island, and back to the city. Late in the evening, there were even some fireworks!'

"And thus the stories went on and on. Every big storm of the last hundred years and every big event anywhere in the world had taken place in New York Harbor. The proud ferry always emerged as the hero, saving, helping, bringing joy to people, always punctual, in every kind of weather—heat of summer, cold of winter—always!

"'We should go out into the open harbor again,' said the small white boat excitedly, 'as we did in times past!'

"'You know that is not possible!' said the big ferry. 'Right in front of us is that red buoy and you know very well that one is not allowed to go where there is a red buoy! Oh, if a green buoy were there, then I would go again, right away. Then I would turn on my big engines, the water would foam around me, all ships would make room for me and we would again be in the middle of New York Harbor, in the midst of all that traffic!'

"'Dong!' A distant clock sounded the time. It was one o'clock. The owl hurried back to its roost.

"The lights on the boats, which had looked like eyes, went out, the windows and shutters closed. 'Haaawwww,' sounded a small yawn. Then all was silent again.

"'Krrrrrrr … queeeeeeek … krrrrrrrr … queeeeek,' was all the noise that the ferry, the little white boat, and the red buoy made—nothing else. The moon had moved lower. I suddenly felt quite cold. Had it all been a dream? I rowed home quickly.

"The next day, I had to leave on a trip. I returned five months later in November. That afternoon, I immediately went back to the Raritan River, got into my little boat, and went to see whether the big ferry was still there. It was now fall. The trees had lost all their leaves. The sky was gray. A cold wind blew over the water.

"A big boat passed me. It had a large crane mounted on top and plenty of scrap iron—the whole boat was full of it. Five men stood on deck, coarsely dressed and dirty. I wondered if they were bandits who had stolen the old iron to sell it as scrap. They really looked dangerous. The boat did not have any markings, so it could not be identified and located later.

"As they reached my ferry, they stopped their ship and looked at it.

"'Let's see if there is anything left on board worth taking along,' said one of the bandits. They were so close to the ferry that he could jump over, that dirty guy. He quickly disappeared into the ferry.

"After a few minutes, he appeared on deck again and called over to his buddies: 'The big engine is still inside. We should take it.'

Now they turned their big crane around to reach over the ferry. The crane easily lifted a large lid on top of the ferry. A big hook on a steel cable was lowered.

You could hear banging and swearing by the man inside the ferry. Then the crane started lifting, and slowly an enormous motor came out of the ferry, still shiny, with oil dripping from the disconnected ends, as if it had been the pulsing heart of the boat only moments ago.

"Before the bandits' boat left, one of the men on board said; 'We'll take that red buoy, too. We can put it in front of our hideaway. Then nobody will dare to come in looking for us.'

"To make room on their already full boat, they threw some old iron overboard. A small green buoy, which they had stolen before somewhere else, was dumped, too. It happened to fall in the water just where the red buoy had been before. What a coincidence!

"I could not watch any longer. I felt so miserable, angry, and helpless in my tiny little fishing boat, alone against five big bandits.

"In no time, they started their ship's engine again and disappeared around the next bend in the river.

"It was only three days until the next full moon. I knew I had to be with the ferry when it came awake again at midnight. Maybe I could comfort her.

"I was there as soon as night fell three days later. It felt cold and lonely. I looked out into the dark emptiness of the water and glided close to my ferry, hiding between the reeds close by.

"'Dong, dong, dong ...' sounded the clock at midnight. A bird called out in the distance, as if crying. The window-eyes of the two boats began to light up faintly. I heard the yawning again, 'Haaaawwwww!'

"The small white boat spoke first again. 'It is turning cold, ferry. Winter is coming. We should move closer together. Together, everything is more bearable.'

"'Yes.' said the ferry, as if in deep thought.

"'Ferry!' cried the small white boat suddenly. "'Ferry, ferry! Look there! The buoy turned green! We can go out again!'

"'Ohhhhhh!' cried the ferry with a sound like I had never heard before—so warm, so full of life and strength. That must have been her voice when she was young and traveled back and forth through the harbor.

"All of a sudden, all shutters opened, all windows were full of light. It was as if the ferry became bigger, as if she were collecting all her strength and power again.

"However, all remained silent.

"Once more, all windows lit up, and an enormous tension ran through the ferry.

"Again, all remained silent.

"Several minutes must have passed. The windows showed no more light. Then, the ferry said in a weak voice, sounding old and empty, 'I cannot go anymore ... never again ... I ... I no longer have my motor.'

"The ferry seemed to rest deeper in the cold, black water, a bit tilted, helplessly stuck in the reeds."

* * * *

My dream had ended there. I paused in writing. What a bitter dream. For many, that's all there is to life. A red buoy stops them all the time. They wait for the green buoy, and if it ever comes, it is too late. But I could not end my story like that. Is there nothing left in life when great expectations are lost? Could there not be peace in accepting life as it is? Writers know that once stories begin, they sometimes take a course of their own—and, thereby, may surprise and give unexpected comfort to the writer themselves. Here it is.

* * * *

Henry continued talking:

"There was a long silence between the boats on the Raritan River that night.

"The small white boat pressed close against the ferry in the dark and the cold. Then it said, 'Ferry!'

"'What is left to say?' answered the ferry with a weak and hardly audible voice.

"'We must have been mooring here for twenty years now,' said the small white boat.

"'Yes,' said the ferry.

"'It was nice whenever you told stories. All these exciting and colorful stories.'

"'Yes,' said the ferry.

"'Why do we have to go out again, then? Why do we have to squeeze through all those strange ships again? Why must we take another trip? Why can't we just rest here, together, where it is so nice and quiet?'

"The small white boat leaned against the big ferry. 'We can be quite happy here. You keep telling me stories, and I'll keep listening.'

"'Dong!' sounded the distant clock, and the magic hour was over."

Henry looked out into the dark and remained silent, as if in deep thought.

His little granddaughter leaned close against him, smiling at him through her tears.

Spring in Princeton

Life can be full of surprises—
and very funny at that

How beautiful is spring in Princeton! The winter storms are gone. The garden turns green. The air is mild. Flowers abound. The songbirds have returned.

My wife, Eva, and I sit on comfortable chairs on the terrace, drink tea, and are happy.

Come to think, there is still a little more to do for me before we leave on a big trip by car across America eight weeks from now. Furthermore, Eva is the volunteer co-chairperson of the yearly town fair, called the Princeton June Fête, a fund-raiser for the local hospital. The Fête will take place in six weeks. Quite a bit has to be coordinated yet. There will be more than twenty different activities for more than the twenty-five thousand visitors expected.

And I, for my part, still plan to do a few small home improvements before we leave.

A few days later:
Nothing is simple in this world. Life has a way of confronting—and con-founding—us with complications. A volunteer on Eva's staff, the one in charge of organizing the most important attraction for the Fête, has disappeared. Nobody can find him. He simply disappeared. Rumor

has it that the task proved too complex for him. That may well be, but no replacement can be found, not at this late hour. To make matters worse, no one knows what arrangements he had already made.

Then, there is the beer supplier, who suddenly demands exclusivity—in other words, the dismissal of his competitor, who happens to be a well-respected citizen of our town. The demand is not acceptable! The whole supplier situation has to be renegotiated!

And how about the new car to be raffled? There aren't enough volunteers to sell tickets on Palmer Square, which is in the center of town. So Eva has to sit there for hours. Sometimes, I sit with her.

Every day, new problems crop up. One day, Eva spent twelve hours on the phone without surfacing for fresh air!

And what about my home improvement projects? The heating oil tank, for instance. We just switched to gas but are not allowed to leave the old, now empty, tank lying there under the ground. It's a whale of a tank—one thou-sand-gallon capacity—under the ground near the entrance at the front of the house. It will sure make a big hole when the monster comes out in a couple of days.

Then there is this new invasion of carpenter ants, which are ten times the size of termites, in the kitchen, in the pantry, in our garden room—all over the place! I now know how the Pharaoh felt when he got hit by one of the plagues. Apparently, the flat roof above the garden room began to leak, getting the wood in the rafters wet, and wet wood is much preferred by termites, these little natural wonders of destruction. It is high time that we have the wooden roof replaced with a sloping copper one—before the exterminator appears. I swiftly locate a good subcontractor to do the work.

Today, Eva declares that it is the custom for all co-chairs of the Fête to invite all the important volunteers on the staff to a luncheon prior to the big day of the fair. Because restaurants are too expensive, she has simply invited fifty people— forty-seven ladies and three gentlemen—to lunch at our home in three weeks. That garden room is the only suitable room for such an occasion. So the roof and carpenter ants must be taken care of by that date.

I recall that the weather in May can be quite warm, which means that for this great occasion we should finally install the air conditioner—something we have been discussing for a couple of years.

More trouble is brewing. For the trip across America through remote wilderness and canyon areas, I had purchased a ten-year-old Chevy Suburban, one of those four-wheel-drive elephants usable as a camper in case we ever get stuck in the middle of nowhere. But the seller can't locate the vehicle's title, and I have already paid him. My son, who is just now attending business school, tells me I was tricked. He could also sell me a few things for which he doesn't have a title.

How about our neighbor's house? He could give it to me for half price. Or the Brooklyn Bridge?

Things get really complicated and a bit funny:
One of our son calls us one day to announce that he wants to come up to see us. Isn't that heartwarming for us parents? When he arrives, we talk for a while, play a game of cards, and he leaves to return home. In times past, our kids quite often had some special concern when they showed up at home. Would there be nothing this time?

Three days later, our son visits us again. I leave Eva alone with him. Sometimes, there is better communication between just the two of them. What do I hear from Eva afterwards? Our son has decided to marry his girlfriend of several years on June 3—only one week before the Fête. And he wants to do it in our backyard!

Things are really getting hectic by now. Our son calls every day to discuss preparations for the wedding. Our future daughter-in-law appears in Princeton to discuss many details personally with Eva. Shall we (*We!* I think to myself) have a stand-up buffet reception or a sit-down meal. What time should the wedding be? And more.

I notice the nice young couple walking through our garden to pick the right spot for the ceremony. Then they depart to go shopping. Later, I hear that they went to a bakery. When a piece of pastry began to slide off the counter, our future daughter-in-law alertly jumped back. Our son was upset because she didn't catch the piece that he had already paid for. The future bride declared loudly that he might as well forget the wedding. She would go home. And she left the store crying, but then stayed at our home with Eva.

A lady from across the street tells us that her son also called once to tell her that he wanted to get married in their backyard within two weeks. The day before that call, her husband had dug up the whole backyard to replant. They had to quickly reseed everything, and fertilize—with double the usual amount—and water three times every day. On the day of the wedding, the first green shoots were just coming out of the ground.

Another neighbor tells us that just before their garden wedding, somebody confused the lawn fertilizer with grass killer. All the grass died two days before the wedding. Her husband took one of the remaining patches of grass to the paint store, bought matching green paint, and sprayed all the dead grass green.

As for our garden ceremony, we still don't know whether the pastor of our church or the mayor of our town will conduct the ceremony. Our future daughter-in-law prefers the pastor, our son the mayor. Finally, the young couple agrees that both dignitaries should perform the ceremony together. I tactfully mention that this could cause problems. Then they agree that the mayor will do the ceremony and that one of our son's brothers will read from the Bible. I decide to buy a video recorder to document this event.

The young couple suggests that all arrangements be festive. Promptly, another neighbor tells us that his wedding was also supposed to be festive: men in tuxedos, ladies in long dresses. The wedding was held in a beautiful park, where a small dam had backed up the creek to form a small, picturesque lake. Unfortunately, this neighbor did not know that, on the same day of his wedding, the local canoe club had organized a big regional rally. It was a hot day and all the canoe club members wore sweaty T-shirts, and they had to get out of their canoes at the dam to drag their boats up into the lake, shouting loud complaints about the extra effort.

Our son complains about the price of a diamond ring. A friend tells us that he, too, bought a really expensive diamond ring for his bride, leaving him with no money to buy a car. After that, they referred to the diamond ring as "the car." And a friend of ours from California reports that when his daughter got married, the young couple exchanged watches instead of rings to be more modern. I just wonder whether those watches beeped every hour.

We still need a photographer. Again, friends come up with a story. At their wedding, a famous photographer came all the way from New York City. After a short time, he was so drunk that he fell asleep on a chair. Fortunately, he had brought a young assistant, who diligently took many pictures. When they were developed, it turned out that most pictures did not show the couple getting married. Instead, they were of the very pretty maid of honor the young photographer had fallen in love with.

Whatever detail of the wedding we discuss with our friends, they immediately tell us a related story. What our son will wear? Something festive, of course. Did we hear the story of Emperor Haile Selassie's visit to Princeton? His majesty was also festively dressed, wearing an imperial hat and a leopard skin draped around his shoulders. When he arrived at the hotel, he was guided to the elevator. Unfortunately, somebody had overlooked the fact that the Shriners were holding their convention on the same day at the same hotel. As the elevator door opened, there stood the great leader of the Shriners, a very big man, with his decorative Fez on his head and a very large leopard skin around his shoulders, which was clearly bigger than Haile Selassie's. Someone quickly pushed a button, the elevator doors closed, and the great Shriner went down into the basement.

Our future daughter-in-law suggests that the groom wear a tuxedo for the wedding. But our son is too frugal to buy a tuxedo to be used only for a wedding and seldom, if ever, afterward. One of his brothers is different. He likes proper attire and does have a tuxedo. So, our son the groom-to-be talks his brother into loaning the tuxedo to him right away for the day of the wedding. However, our future charming daughter-in-law has spoiled our son with good food (sic!), so he has gained some pounds. The buttons of his brother's tuxedo will need to be moved in order to fit. But that brother won't arrive until the evening before the wedding. Come to think of it, I still have an old tuxedo from my business days. The buttons would certainly be set wide enough.

Our son and his bride tell us that they have some time for a short vacation now, but not after the wedding. They decide to take their honeymoon trip to the remote jungle of Costa Rica now, two weeks before the wedding.

Incidentally, at 11:00 p.m. on the night before their departure, a four-page computer file is mailed to us, listing everything we can do for them during their absence. They even call from a stopover airport, asking whether we had received the list. Yes, we did. Yes, all was quite readable on the computer. They say they will call us in a few days, which happens to be Mother's Day! Touching! They also say that if they find a fax machine in Costa Rica, we can let them know what all was done already from the list—so that they can relax more during their trip.

The brother from Chicago calls once in a while just to say hello—and to check up on our progress with the list. He had received a copy of the list, along with a request to monitor our progress. I admire the level of organized efficiency that our sons have attained. Funny, when they were small, wasn't it that kind of efficient monitoring from their parents that they had so much disliked?

The title for the Chevy Suburban still has not arrived. By now, I have quite a bit of repair and service work invested in the vehicle. The purchase of a cheap old car can be an expensive proposition.

Now, we get into some real problems:
I learn that our thousand-gallon oil tank, which we are going to have removed, is bigger than I thought and will disrupt the walkway up to the front door of our house. Furthermore, the excavation will not take place until next week. If need be, the fifty luncheon guests invited by Eva will pass by the garbage cans and come in through the narrow back door, which needs a new coat of paint.

The subcontractor for the leaking roof over the garden room, however, shows up right on schedule. He quickly removes the large skylight and some beams around it. Then he covers the gaping hole in the ceiling with some boards and supports it with old two-by-fours, nicely centered in the middle of the room. He cannot finish the job because he is committed to work on another contract tomorrow. He might possibly come back in a week, but he is not sure.

The roofer, who is supposed to put the copper roof on the new beams, has also disappeared. He took a ten-day vacation to play tennis in Florida.

The air-conditioning unit "will soon (!) be delivered by the manufacturer"— also in two weeks. Installation is promised promptly. Will it be ready for the luncheon party, or for the wedding, or not at all?

A big rainstorm, predicted to last for several days, approaches, and a workman from the roof subcontractor shows up and puts an enormous blue tarp over the opening in the ceiling of the garden room.

The other subcontractor—the one meant to remove the oil tank—calls to say that he can't do anything until the rain ends. That will be the day before the big luncheon, if not the day of the luncheon.

The subcontractor for the roof should be ready to come back then, too. Can we suspend him over the tables while fifty guests eat? He might finish in time for the wedding, though.

But that still leaves the air conditioner.

The mayor of Princeton calls and asks whether we will have a two-ring wedding or a one-ring wedding. There are different ceremonies for each. I can well imagine a two-ring wedding, but how would it be in a one-ring wedding, if one person alone gets married—to him or herself? Eva and I look at each other and don't know the answer. Our son and future daughter-in-law cannot be reached, because they're in Costa Rica.

The papers for my car are now definitely promised for next Tuesday. Meanwhile, I have added new shock absorbers and excellent new tires. That cost me almost as much as what I paid for the whole car, which—come to think of it— has traveled over one hundred thousand miles already.

Pause—or "the Eye of the Storm":
The heavy rains arrive right on schedule. Apparently, that's the only thing that goes according to schedule. The blue tarp does not hold tight, and we have plenty of water on the floor in the garden room and in the kitchen. I hope it will kill all the carpenter ants.

Low and behold, what do I see? The ants are all climbing up the walls. Only one still floats in the middle of the water on a small piece of plastic. Noah on his modern ark! I blow softly until the ant reaches a wall and can safely climb out. It certainly will have its own story to tell!

In this rain, none of the workers show up. It has been raining steadily for two days already.

Eva develops a stomach flu and stays in bed.

She sleeps for twenty-four hours.

When she wakes up, she asks me to bring her some tea.
I sit in a comfortable chair at her bedside.
The house is very quiet.
All you hear is the sound of computer keys as I write this report.
The blooming garden looks enchanting in the returning sun.
How beautiful is spring in Princeton!

Full action resumes—crescendo to finale:

All of a sudden, Eva recovers and all the workers return to their jobs—unbe-lievable!

Within a few very, very hectic days, the garden room gains proper cover, the fuel tank gets lifted out of the ground, the hole is temporarily filled, and the air conditioner is installed sufficiently to cool the house.

The wedding takes place only a few days later—on a cloudy day. But when the beautiful bride is ready to walk down the lawn toward the arch of flowers where the wedding ceremony takes place, the sky clears and a wonderful ray of sunshine illuminates her elegant figure and smiling face. May the young couple's life always be that happy.

Just one week later, after another hundred phone calls and twenty team meetings, the Fête takes place as scheduled. Thousands of visitors appear and are pleased—with a good financial result for our hospital.

All of a sudden, we receive the papers for the new camper—and, another week later, we leave Spring in Princeton for a very happy vacation.

Happy Wildlife in Princeton

*

Surprise encounters—some resonance—and a smile remains

*

Princeton is a quiet university town with a beautiful campus, a small business district, and suburban living for twenty-five thousand residents. Where is there room for wildlife? Not much on campus. The curriculum is too demanding for the students to get wild. The scientists are too involved in their quests for the next Nobel Prize. But look at the fringes of our town. There deer herds move in from the surrounding forests to harvest the flower gardens in town. Look above, where drifting turkey vultures circle silently high in the air or delta formations of Canadian geese migrate swiftly by, their cries of distant freedom occasionally still heard through the night. But the animals that live in town are adjusted to suburban life, closer to us humans. Who can still doubt their capability for consciousness, thought, and emotions after observing them long enough with empathy? Let me write about some of my animal friends who live on our own property.

*

The Squirrel

*

When I write, I sit at an octagonal bay window, where a stately Japanese maple provides shade in the summer. This tree also provides seeds for the squirrels to feed on. By now, one of those squirrels knows me—the same one that pokes deep holes into my otherwise beautiful front lawn to hide its reserves. I tell it to get a safe deposit box at the bank in town but it only tilts its head and scampers on. Sometimes, that squirrel climbs to a branch really close to my window. There it sits for many minutes observing me writing at the computer keyboard. Finally it looks as if it wants to ask me something.

"Why do you always scratch at the same place with your paws where you don't find anything to eat?" it begins. "That's not the way to support yourself and save for hard times or old age!" it continues in an almost patronizing way. Had it heard me talking to my sons?

"You must apply yourself, jump around, search here and there where it makes sense. That's the way to find good things!" and off it jumps—just to the next branch—munching on some seeds and looking over its shoulder to make sure that I saw and got the point.

It does that three or four times, always returning to my window. Then it sighs, gives up on me, and goes after its own business, leaving me behind to keep scratching the old keyboard. In gratitude, I put some walnuts out on the ground under the maple tree.

In late fall, when the frost comes as soon as the early nights approach, our roles are inverted. A mild light emanates from my warm office. Then, the squirrel comes up and sits there, looking and thinking, its head slightly tilted, again. But as if to prove that it is not all on the wrong side, it jumps down to the lawn, retrieves a nut from one of those holes, and disappears in its nest of fall leaves high above in a tree—not without looking at me over its shoulder one last time in triumph.

*

The Crows

*

This year, the local crow family, part of a larger clan in town, built its nest right above our back porch, high up in an ash tree. We observed the coming and going as the nest was built and then the quieter time of incubating the eggs. Finally the small heads of the crow chicks peeked over the edge of the nest. The parents had a hard time keeping the chicks well enough fed.

Last Saturday evening we had a spaghetti and chicken dinner on that porch. The crow parents looked on with great envy; there was so much food on the table we could not finish it all. How could we live so comfortably in our house knowing that those poor crow chicks would go hungry up in their nest?

I got a paper plate, loaded it with some spaghetti, put some nice pieces of chicken on top, and placed it quite a ways down the sloping lawn, where I thought it would be found easily.

It took the crow parents only one overflight to spot the food. Both parents perched on high branches of the spruce and black walnut trees in back of our garden and vocalized their excitement loudly—but too careful to fly down to the food immediately.

More than ten minutes passed in the crows' careful approach of their prey. They always looked nervously at us as they descended slowly to lower branches. Any movement or sound from us made them quickly return to higher ground.

Finally, both sat on the lawn, though still at a safe distance from the tempting plate. One or the other approached the plate with careful steps, ogled it with tilted head, and retreated once more to safety with a jump.

Then came the breakthrough. One of the crows—was it the male or the female?—came close enough to the plate to pick at the food and tear out a spaghetti noodle like a long, white wiggling worm. Soon the other one came and made away with a good morsel of chicken meat.

Once they got to the plate, there was no more holding the line. The crows' beaks dug deep into the pile, and the happy parents flew up with big strokes of their wings, heavily loaded like cargo planes, to the nest in the tree, where the expecting chicks had observed everything with great longing from the rim of their lofty home.

The plate was empty before the night arrived, and everything turned happily silent in the nest. I know those moments from when our children grew up with us, and we enjoyed the yearly tax refund celebration dinner at the Alchemist and Barrister or Rusty Scupper restaurant in town. The kids even took leftovers home for another late supper.

We liked the display of natural behavior from our tenants on the tree—and we felt good about having helped them out a bit. So we put more food out, almost daily. One evening, we ate so late that it was dark when we finished. The crows are not night foragers. We heard their complaints in the dark, but we put the plate of food for them under the table on the porch to keep it away from the prowlers of the dark, the opossums and the you-don't-know-whats—specifically, away from the neighbor's cat.

Shortly after six in the morning, when the sun had barely risen, throwing its wonderful golden light on the tops of the summer-green trees, we were awakened by the angriest rebuke projected at us by one of the crow parents, sitting just outside our bedroom window at a place where he or she could see us asleep in bed.

There would be no more rest until I got up and—still in my pajamas; what a sight!—retrieved the loaded plate from under the porch table and put it out where the crows rightfully expected it.

By that time, the chicks had left the nest and sat only a few feet away from the plate. The parents shuttled back and forth between the plate and the chicks. How good can life be?

Furthermore, word had gotten around to the larger clan about the high life in our backyard. First one uncle or aunt, then at least ten of them with their youngsters, appeared and wanted to be part of public welfare.

I have some experience with people, and thus stated that we were doing the crows a disservice. The chicks would not learn to find food for themselves, and the clan would lose its neglected territory to other clans—not to mention the crutch effect of too much help. From that day on, the food supply was cut off!

Wild complaints from the crow clan continued for weeks. I never told anybody that I secretly continued to put out some food for quite some time. How could we live so comfortably in our house, knowing that those poor crows would go hungry?

The crows still come to the feeding spot from time to time and vocalize nostalgically, especially when they notice me watching.

*

The Bird in the Bush

*

I like to walk through our backyard and sit on a bench we placed under a canopy of branches of a wide and tall bush on the left side of the down-sloping lawn. From late spring on, I am usually greeted by a little bird with a melancholic voice.

"Yeeeeeeeeaaaaaahhhh!" it softly cries, starting with a high pitch and ending with a much lower pitch.

I have learned to answer with a "yeeeeeeeeaaaaaahhh!" of my own.

That's just what my little friend was hoping for: a little conversation.

And so it goes, "yeeeeeeeeaaaaaahhh," "yeeeeeeeeaaaaaahhh," back and forth for some time.

The little bird changes position in the bush, starting on my right side and moving to my left, slowly getting closer until it's finally calling from close behind my back. But a wrong movement—or maybe a missed pitch—makes it quickly withdraw again. I have seen it only once when turning around—feeling like Orpheus—and it flew away immediately, not to come back again that day.

The garden is very quiet most of the time. But when I come to that bush, the "yeeeeeeeeaaaaaahhh, yeeeeeeeeaaaaaahhh" starts again.

Lately, I have tried to add a somewhat happier sound into our exchange. Sometimes it seems to work. But the attempt at a sparkle of rhythm is definitely rejected. Life in the darkness of the bush seems to have a melancholic tune.

Now it is winter. Only some snowbirds, chickadees, and an occasional woodpecker come to our bird feeder.

I can't wait to see spring and my little friend return, as it has done for several years by now.

Let me already call out a welcoming "yeeeeeeeeaaaaaahhh!" for the New Year to you.

*

The Mice

*

We have a guest "cottage" in back of our house, and we don't want you to call it a converted garage! There is beige carpeting on the floor, a Chinese dragon kite hanging between the beams, a nice bed for our guests, and even a reproduction of a Hudson River School painting of wonderful mountain scenery on the wall behind the bed. The bed's mattress is covered with a friendly Amish quilt, and under it are two soft pillows (we do accept married couples, mind you!).

The cottage is very quiet, but guests have occasionally mentioned rustling noises coming from in between the beams. How about that? No, there is no ghost that walks around carrying his head under his arm, a uniformed veteran of Wash-ington's Battle of Princeton in 1777, waiting for his beloved Hessian sweetheart to come and bury him.

Once, we expected a lady guest late in the fall. I wanted to be sure that there was no problem with that noise, so I stayed in the cottage for a while at dusk, keeping myself very quiet. I even held a camera to take a picture of whatever appeared. Yes, I did hear a very faint, muffled noise from the direction of the bed. But the noise was so faint, and there was nothing to be discerned on or under or behind the bed, that I did not raise any fuss about it. I didn't even invent a new story about the noise to get the family excited.

Eva, my wife, had to prepare the bed before the guest arrived. What did she find? Right under one of the pillows, she found a nicely arranged, generous cache of wild seeds.

"Mice!" she screamed.

I ran to see what she had found.

What should we do? I know from experience that people react quite differently to animals, depending on how they look. A rat is ugly and rejected right away. A hamster is cute. A gray house mouse is also not acceptable. But the white-bellied field mouse with a tan pelt, as common in the New Jersey wilds, is so pretty that it can be found in toy stores reproduced as a stuffed little animal for children to coddle.

I got a trap. Sure enough, I caught a mouse. It was one of those cute and beautiful little field mice. The matter seemed resolved, particularly as the rustling noises were not heard any longer.

But what to do with the cache that the mice needed to get through winter? It was cleaned out, the bed was shampooed, a French lavender perfume from our time in Cannes was added, and our guest did not learn about that once hidden treasure—enjoying our "elegant accommodation."

But then, we put a bag of grass seed into the remaining storage area of the garage with ready access to the garden outside or the beams of the cottage next to it.

The mice returned the courtesy by staying away from the bed, preferring to stay closer to the bag of seed.

Sometimes I wish I were nocturnal and small enough to visit with the mice and celebrate the good times with them.

I would throw a party—right on top of those pillows—dancing, feasting, and all!

But I would clean up afterwards.

Did you hear that, you wild mice?

*

The Rabbit

*

We have a rabbit in our backyard that we call "Bunny," as usual. Bunny is a loner. Only once in a while, in spring, Bunny appears with very small baby bunnies. But those disappear as they grow up. Or are they captured by the owl? Only our good old Bunny always remains.

Bunny is well behaved, normally eating only the grass on the lawn. One summer, when we had a severe drought and all the grass turned gray or brown, Bunny got up on her hindquarters and ate the blooms of our white flowers in the shaded area of the garden. Eva, my wife, was upset. I scolded Bunny und put out some fresh salad for her—even a cup with water—that the other animals drank at night. But I also put out a trap, loaded with all kinds of succulent things in it. Bunny, however—the one that always looks so naïve—was too smart to get into it.

As time went by, we all got used to each other. Bunny did not hide any longer when we came into the garden. We could approach her up to just a few steps away if we walked slowly.

We told our four-year-old granddaughter, Christina, in California about Bunny. She was excited and wanted to come over right away. When Christina finally came to visit with us a few months later, she asked immediately about Bunny.

We walked into the backyard with Christina and—we couldn't believe it our-selves—Bunny was there, waiting for her. Bunny sat in the lower part of the lawn, munching on grass.

Christina wanted to run out and greet Bunny, but we told her that she had to walk very slowly and not talk, so as not to scare Bunny. It was a wonderful sunny day. All the flowers were blooming, and there walked, step by step carefully down the lawn toward her new friend, our little blond granddaughter.

Bunny was insecure and acted as if she did not see Christina. Bunny just went on munching grass. But I noticed that Bunny's head turned toward the child and her eyes fixed on Christina.

When Christina was just a few steps from Bunny—walking very, very slowly—Bunny raised herself up on her hind quarters, her ears up, her forepaws lifted, and looked straight at Christina. Our granddaughter stopped mid-step, one foot still raised behind her from the last step, both hands lifted slightly sideways in suspense. She smiled with bright eyes at Bunny. How could Bunny resist? She looked as if she smiled, too. What a picture to behold!

Just then a loud noise came from one of the neighbor's gardens.

Faster than the eye could follow, Bunny disappeared between some low plants. Christina remained standing alone in her lovely pose in the sunshine on the lawn. Had she just experienced a real fairy tale? Had she also just experienced reality?

Slowly she turned to us, half smiling and half crying, and was taken up in the arms of her mother.

Bunny came back a while later when we were all gone. I could see Bunny from the house as she looked around where little Christina had stood.

Since then, I have not seen Bunny for more than half a year.

*

Yes, there are also deer in Princeton—many hundreds of them. But that is neither a funny nor a happy story. That is not just the question of the deer eating all the flowers and decorative bushes in people's gardens. There are all those car on deer collisions. More than a hundred of them, in some years. The cars get dented, sometimes skid into a ditch or tree. People usually don't get hurt. But the deer get severely hurt. If they don't die on the spot, they may have to be relieved of their pain by being euthanized. Deer are not that good at jumping fences either. They can jump high, but apparently they cannot see wire-mesh fences very well. If they misjudge the height of such a fence, they don't land properly on their feet after the jump and may break one of their tender legs. We had this happen the other day in our own backyard. The suffering animal was barely able to move to the center of our garden. It lay down at the spot with the most beautiful view of all the shrubs and flowers and gave up the struggle.

Two Lives

Could it be the story of many marriages—
or the solution for some problems?

*

A good marriage is like a piece of art, or quite often, like a circus act on the high wire. And it's not easy to stay up there. You and your marriage partner develop certain habits, certain mannerisms. Some may be funny at the beginning, but some begin to irritate as time goes on, and some are just plain boring. Did you expect your marriage to be like that? One day you meet another couple. Diagonally across, you find the other marriage partner more interesting than your own. But all your friends tell you what a fabulous marriage partner you already have. Can you and your own partner not see that? Can you not just leave the somewhat worn tracks and snap out of irritation or boredom? Can you and your partner not simply jump over to a new and better set of tracks, at the same time—how else would it work?—then move along much happier—as you both once wanted to be? That reminds me of Tom and Evelyn.

*

Phase 1: Together in Harmony on One Track

I met Tom and Evelyn in 1977, in Santa Clara, California. They were both in their early thirties, slender, attractive—he was blond; she was dark-haired—and well dressed. He was the chief accountant at a small electronics company. She was a teacher. They had met in high school in Fresno, in the Central Valley, and had married soon after high school. In those years, many youngsters married before fully developing their own personalities, before getting to know each other. But, then, also in those years of their youth, their minds were filled with love.

During Tom and Evelyn's courtship, each did everything to be attractive to the other. They did everything they could think of to make the other happy. They lived with much laughter, like living on a different level of existence from ours, as never before … or ever again?

Tom had always been fascinated by numbers. He liked the accuracy and security of numbers, so he went into accounting. Evelyn had been fascinated by learning and the finer things in life. When she became a teacher, she tried to help young people make something of their lives and reach for higher goals.

Their marriage was harmonious, though without excitement. Children did not arrive. Both worked hard, and they had an impeccable home. Could they not have remained happy? Everybody liked them. Others considered their marriage a model one.

Phase 2: The Tracks Diverge

Tom's World:

Tom's colleagues considered him a nice guy. He was always friendly and reliable. His job did not require much creativity, rather the keeping of a low profile. It demanded none of the self-assurance that the engineers in the company had or of the ingratiating ways of the salesmen.

Tom worked long hours, quite often coming home late. When he got home, he just wanted to relax. He often watched TV—mostly sports.

The ideal wife for him would have been a tender woman, someone who wanted merely to care for him.

But that was not Evelyn's main attribute.

It wasn't long before Tom sensed that their marriage was cooling off. He learned to be content and to withdraw somewhat into his own world. But the situation weighed more and more heavily on him. The sparkle of life disappeared. He let himself be dragged down. He no longer cared how he looked or what he said to Evelyn. He lost interest in what few hobbies he had. In short, he felt as if he were locked in a cage.

Then something surprising happened.

Tom dreamed that Evelyn was his ideal wife again, full of tenderness, caring for him, always being there for him—a true partner in life. The dream became a second reality for him. He began to live in two worlds.

Evelyn's World:

Evelyn's colleagues also considered her to be nice. She was always friendly and reliable. Her work demanded much creativity, some self-assurance, and being at ease with people—both children and their parents.

She aspired to the higher and finer things in life. When she returned home in the afternoon, she often read a good book while listening to music.

For her, the ideal husband would have been a man who was interesting, dynamic, and somewhat elegant. But those were not qualities Tom possessed, as she well knew.

It wasn't long before Evelyn sensed that their marriage was cooling off. But she adjusted and learned to be content. She withdrew a little into her own world. The spark of life had gone. She let herself be dragged down a little. She didn't care how she looked any longer or what she said to Tom. She gained some weight. And, finally, she too felt as though she were in a cage.

Then something surprising happened.

Evelyn dreamed that Tom was her ideal husband again: full of intellectual interests, dynamic, a little elegant, always there for her—a true partner in life. The dream became a second reality for her. She began to live in two worlds.

Phase 3: Each Track Splits Once More

Tom's Real World:

Tom got up early in the morning. Evelyn often slept later, because her classes started later. He prepared breakfast for himself and sat at the table in his undershirt, reading the newspaper. When it was time to go, he put on a dress shirt and necktie and drove to work.

Evenings were not much different. Tom came home late from work. If Evelyn had not eaten already, he helped to prepare dinner. They ate at the kitchen table.

Afterwards, Tom washed the dishes. Later, while Evelyn corrected students' papers, he watched TV—sports or financial news, perhaps a romantic love story with a little excitement.

Sometimes, he longed for a woman he could really love. It was no wonder that he started to look at other women. When he met an especially attractive one, he really turned on his charm and became even more critical of his own wife.

Tom's Dreams:

In his fantasy, Tom saw himself getting up in the morning. He found the breakfast table already set and the meal prepared. Evelyn stood there, smiling at him. He kissed her before he sat down. Later, they cleaned the table together and went hand-in-hand through their little garden before he kissed her good-bye and drove off. She waved for as long as she could see him.

In the evening, on the way home, he looked forward to seeing Evelyn again. His wife would certainly have prepared a little refreshment for him.

When he reached home, she opened the door for him. She had been waiting for him to come home. She really looked chic—what a radiant face she had! You had to love this woman. He tenderly drew her close and gave her a kiss.

They sat together for a long time that evening and talked about their work.

Evelyn's Real World:

Evelyn no longer got up early, because classes started at 9:00 a.m. Since Tom usually left early, she prepared breakfast for herself, efficiently and swiftly. She checked some textbooks she intended to use and even telephoned some parents who wanted to see her that day.

Their evenings were not much different.

Evelyn often returned early from school. When she knew that Tom would be late, she ate dinner alone. Otherwise, she helped him prepare dinner. They ate at the kitchen table.

After dinner, she went back to correcting students' papers. Occasionally, she read a good book—perhaps a romantic love story with a little excitement.

Sometimes, she longed for a man she could really love. It was no wonder that she started to look at other men. When she met an especially attractive one, she really turned on her charm and became even more critical of her own husband.

Evelyn's Dreams:

In her fantasy, Evelyn saw how they had breakfast together. Tom looked so elegant in his new business suit. Why hadn't they made him a vice president at the company? While they had coffee, they talked animatedly about their respective tasks for the day and about the interesting people they would meet. After Tom left, the house appeared empty to her.

At home in the evening, she looked forward to his return from work. Her husband would certainly bring her some flowers again.

When she heard his car arrive, she quickly opened the door for him and stepped out with a radiant face. How elegant he looked, and what an interesting man he was! You had to love this man! How happy she was when he drew her into his arms.

They sat together for a long time that evening and talked to each other about their work.

Phase 4: Jumping to the New Track

Tom's New Mind-set:

Then the unexpected happened: suddenly, Tom couldn't distinguish dream from reality any longer.

He was on his way home from work and thought that his dream wife was waiting for him.

So he actually stopped at a flower shop and bought a small, beautiful bunch of flowers. Before he walked up to his house, he combed his hair and checked his looks in the car mirror. Then, with elastic steps, he walked to the door.

Evelyn's New Mind-set:

Then the unexpected happened: suddenly, Evelyn couldn't distinguish dream from reality any longer.

She had arrived home early and thought that her dream husband would come home to her soon.

She actually prettied herself up a little, brought in some flowers from the garden, and prepared a little refreshment for her husband. When she heard his car pull up, she arranged her hair and checked her looks in the mirror by the door. She put on some nice music and opened the door with a radiant face.

Phase 5: In Harmony on the New Track

Together:

They hardly dared to sink into each other's arms—to realize their dream, to sense the spark of life again, to be their better selves again, to be loved again, to have found somebody to love and to share laughter with. What joy and freedom! They could not speak at first. Tom kissed Evelyn lightly, and she blushed. Then she pulled him into the house, took his briefcase out of his hand, and led him to the dining table where the refreshment waited for him.

"You are wonderful!" he said.

"I love you!" she answered.

"You have such a radiant face today!" he said. "What was so good in school today that you look so happy?"

"Nothing special. Tell me about your day, my love," she answered.

*

I've seen Toms and Evelyns a number of times since then.
Sometimes, things went well.
Sometimes not.
But now, occasionally, I buy a bunch of flowers on my way home.
Then my "Evelyn" drops whatever she is doing, and we laugh together,
grateful for each other.

The Wall

*

Did death approach the salesman—but joy and love result?

*

As usual, we spent the summer at our vacation apartment in Provence, close to the beach. We went swimming in the mornings, read books in the shade of the garden during the days, and had dinner at one of the picturesque little villages up in the hills— Mougins, Valbonne, Cabris. Life was pleasant and light, almost elegant.

Then something unusual happened. I woke up one morning with the last vision of a bad dream still clear in my mind. Somehow, I had run into a stone wall and remembered only the moment that my head was going to hit the wall. I could then feel the unforgiving hardness of the granite stone as I expected to die.

When I came fully awake, I had the certain foreboding that my life would come to an end during the approaching fall. It took me all day to collect myself enough to speak to my family about this dream and the feeling of approaching death. When I finally told them, they all laughed, telling me to cheer up and not to be superstitious.

Over the next few weeks, however, the following story developed in my mind and gave me peace. Now, many years later—still alive—I write the story down.

*

Jacques lived in an insignificant suburb of a town—I don't know which—in Provence. Those suburbs all look alike: streets lined with four-story, gray or brick apartment buildings, all close together, with small shops at street level.

Jacques made deliveries. He drove a small old van and brought the merchan-dise—I forgot what it was—in small, prepared packages to various stores, all in proper sequence, through all the streets in his quarter of town. He had figured out how he had to drive, beginning with the closest street going from right to left, then the street behind that, going from left to right, and so on; in a serpentine pattern to the end of the last street. Then he would return home.

One morning, Jacques woke up from a dream with a jolt, sweating and confused. In his dream, he had been driving along on his daily round, when he ran into a stone wall. He distinctly remembered the moment when his head was going to hit the wall. He still sensed the unforgiving hardness of the granite stone as he expected to die. The wall was made of those midsize boulders you find in riverbeds. Jacques remembered every detail of the dream, even the big gray stone his head was going to hit. That was the end.

Jacques got up, pale and distraught, and left for his daily round without talking to his wife or daughter. His wife watched him drive off with a sad, questioning expression on her face.

He traveled back and forth through all those streets on the day of the dream and the next day.

On the third day, however, something even more unusual occurred. Jacques saw exactly the same wall that had appeared in his dream. There it was just across the street as he made a right turn on his way home. He believed he recognized every stone on the gray surface constructed of granite river boulders. There was the large stone his head was supposed to hit.

He did not talk to his wife or daughter at home. He ate little, then left home again "to take care of some business." He paced for hours through the streets in the dark of the night. What sense was there in having lived his life? What sense did it make to keep on living? What was it all about? He was always working— for a sparse apartment, a simple wife, and his thin little daughter? To get drunk was meaningless. To kill himself—what that stone would do anyway—was equally meaningless. Too bleak, too bottomless was everything for him to enjoy life any longer. Just pass the time, until the unavoidable would happen. He felt cut off from the world, separated as though by a glass wall, on his way to a far horizon—a feeling that some newly afflicted cancer patients experience.

Returning home, Jacques found everything dark. His wife and daughter had gone to bed. He touched his wife lightly, not knowing why. Did he subconsciously hope that she could break the spell or give him warmth? His wife did not react. He went to bed and slept abysmally deep. The next morning, he woke up before the others and left for his last trip—so he thought.

Jacques wanted to follow his usual course once more in his old van. He had calculated precisely at what time he would arrive at that wall. But today he moved faster, at first without even calling out his usual "Bonjour. Ça va?" to the shopkeepers.

But then his mood changed inexplicably. He drove more slowly, saluting his customers again. He answered their questions and, finally, began the usual small talk.

An unbelievable inner freedom began to release all his stress. He began to feel like he was floating above real life. Now he saw the light in the sunny streets of Provence again that is so much appreciated by the famous painters. He perceived all the people in the streets: the women and the playing children.

Jacques made his delivery to the last store. Then he started on his way home— toward that wall, toward the end of all pain in life, toward a new, free world— where his wife and daughter might one day join him.

He stopped at a flower shop to buy a bunch of spring flowers for his wife and a gift for his child. How useless! How free he actually already felt!

As Jacques approached the corner around which the wall expected him, he heard an approaching ambulance from the distance. Was the siren sounding for him? New stress caught him, stronger than before. Sweat came to his forehead. Then he felt cool again. There he was, separated from all the others, alone with his destiny on a predetermined path. For the last few seconds, he kept his head high, even with a smile—as ancient Greek statues show on dying warriors.

The ambulance reached him just as he turned the corner heading toward the wall with full abandon.

A large crowd of people stood around a tall piece of construction equipment. The wall was nowhere to be seen. Only moments before, it had been demolished, and that had caused an accident. Nothing serious, though.

Jacques drove on, as if dreaming. Was he still in the real world? Was he still alive in this sunlight with all those people? Was he on his way home to his wife and daughter?

Jacques laughed out loud. He overflowed with life, maybe even with joy. He drove up to his home with panache and honked so his wife and daughter would know he was there. He saluted the windows, waving the flowers and the gift.

When his wife and daughter came out, he took them into his arms and held them for a long, long time.

The Colorful Ball

*

A story for our young grandchildren, Christina and Scott

*

Did you ever wonder where stories come from? Some are just dreams. But others really happen around you all the time. You must just have the open eyes or mind, and the right feeling in your heart to see and understand the stories. One day, you may see a ball roll along the street. It may be just a ball running along the street. But when you see it right and really understand the ball, then all of a sudden you may feel that there actually is a story. That happened to me just a few days ago. Let me tell you how it was.

*

We live on Westcott Road in Princeton, New Jersey. There are many tall trees on our street and nice green lawns in front of all the friendly houses.

One evening, a few days ago, I went for a long walk. It was very windy. As I walked home, I could already see our house at the end of the road.

But what else did I see some distance in front of me? It was a colorful, little plastic ball bouncing along the street, driven by the wind. The ball was one of those multicolored, inflatable, plastic balls that you sometimes play with on the beach—yellow and red and green and blue.

The ball bounced along, from one side of the street to the other. Sometimes it stopped for a moment, as if it were lost and did not know where to go.

I walked faster, and soon I had caught up with the little ball.

As I came close, the wind must have changed. The little ball turned around, as if it had heard me coming, and slowly bounced toward me. It stopped close to my feet, and I thought it was looking at me. Did the little ball want to ask me something? Had the little ball gotten lost? Did it now want to ask me where its home was, which way it had to go?

I didn't know what to say. So I walked away, and the little ball looked quite sad. Then it tried to follow me, slowly, as if it were tired. But I walked faster than it could bounce along.

As I kept walking, I thought that the little ball must certainly belong to some children. I remembered that a new family with children had arrived on our street just a few days earlier. They had moved into the house I had walked by a minute ago.

So, I turned around and walked back to the little ball. I picked it up and said, "Little ball, I will carry you back. But then, you must sit still and wait until the children come to look for you."

That's what I did. I carried the ball back to where a nice bush stood on one of the lawns. That bush could protect the ball from the wind so the ball would really stay there and not roll away again.

"Good-bye, little ball," I said, "Wait here. I hope the children find you before it turns dark."

Then I walked down the street to our home. I went in and had dinner. Later, when it was already night, I looked out the door to see how the weather was. What did I see? I could not believe it! That little, colorful ball was there. It must have been blown along the street to follow me and now it was sitting right next to our door, as if waiting to be let in!

What could I do? I picked it up and carried it in.

Next morning, after we had breakfast, I said to the ball, "Now you must go home." So I carried it back to the other end of the street toward the house where I hoped the new children lived.

I was smart. Before setting it down, I let some air out of the ball. That way the ball was not as round anymore. It could not roll very well, and the wind could not drive it away so easily. The poor little half-deflated ball looked wrinkled and old—just as I sometimes look in the mirror in the morning; after all, I am sev-enty-five years old.

I left the ball behind, sitting there somewhat heavily on the lawn—not much bounce in it any longer.

I went home. I was quite sad that I didn't have the friendly colorful ball around any longer. Would the children find it where I had left it sitting?

I looked out our door many times that day, hoping to see the ball. If it had come just once more, I would have been glad, and I would have taken it in. I would have blown it up nicely, so it would look young again. Then I would have carried it up to the big playroom in the attic where all the other playthings and toys are, always waiting for you.

The next day, I went back to see what had happened to the little ball. It was no longer where I had put it. But later in the day, I saw some very happy children run along the street.

Every morning now, when I look into the mirror, I still think of the little ball, how I had left it sitting on that lawn.

But then I also think of you. You would have blown the ball up again, so that it was young and round and could happily bounce along ever after.

*

Now, go out for a walk. Look around. Do you see something? Maybe you will see a ball rolling. But maybe you will see another child walking along. If you really see what happens—and if you understand in your heart how the other child feels— then, maybe you have found a new story to tell.

Please call me and tell me your story as soon as you can.

When a Door Opened …

*

and a new light came into their lives!

*

A tribute to our friends

*

I used to work in Southern California in a fully air-conditioned building without windows. Inside, the neon lights illuminated the linearly arranged workbenches and all the machines. When the workday was over and employees began to leave, the heavy steel door opened for a few moments and the light of the bright California sun came in. When I left, I saw the green, tree-covered hills behind the factory building. Then, driving home, I saw the wide and wonderful, blue Pacific Ocean and the beautifully curving Santa Monica Bay. What a blessing if a door opens on our life and lets new light come in. Most of our lives do not run along the same track or drift slowly to new directions. Sometimes, at a certain moment, a door opens, and a new light falls onto our lives—as if giving us a new life! Leaving high school and entering college was such a moment for me. Or leaving college and starting a real job with interesting work and good colleagues. Much to my surprise, the beginning of retirement was such a moment for me and for many people, but, unfortunately, it is not for all. Let me talk about my friends who can be role models for many.

*

Paul and Marie lived in Hossegor, a fashionable seaside resort on the Atlantic coast of southern France. They were both in their late fifties. She was petite, with dark eyes and black hair, and a radiant charm. He was a little taller, with gray eyes, rather a type of northern France, and a bit reserved.

They started a small travel agency. Through hard work over many years of their younger life, they established themselves against fierce competition. They always worked many hours every day together in their office, often until late into the night, even on weekends, knowing that only very good work would provide them with loyal customers and success.

After a while, they were able to buy a pretty little apartment in a modern building with a balcony overlooking a large and beautiful, green atrium that featured an undulating lawn, some decorative bushes all around, some trees here and there, a small pond in the middle, and even a decorative fountain.

Inside their apartment, everything was very tidy, yet a bit artistic. There were some nice pictures on the walls—dreams of beauty in nature—and on a glass shelf, Paul's collection of toy locomotives, symbols of his dreams of exciting travel.

Thus went week after week and year after year. Don't you have to be grateful for a decent life and harmony?

Eventually, they began to think of retirement—if only they could sell their business at a good price—and hoped for a quiet life in their little apartment.

One day they went to an art exhibit in town. A small picture showed a view of some scenery they knew very well, but they agreed that the picture was not very well done. As they left the show, they passed a stand selling art supplies. Marie stopped and looked, obviously interested. Paul, ever the gentleman, purchased some colors, some brushes, and a canvas for Marie. What a wonderful day! Marie kissed Paul, and they went home hand-in-hand.

After only two weekends, Marie produced quite an acceptable little picture of the same scenery, only a bit nicer. The two promptly hung it in their office, where it earned the applause of several customers. They explained to them that it provided a dream of nature in their matter-of-fact office world.

When the end of the business year came, work overwhelmed them, and Paul and Marie had no time for any distractions. But later, as the beautiful spring of the southern climate progressed, Marie returned to her painting and created two more pictures in quick succession.

Paul took great pleasure in Marie's work. Being a practical person and in order to contribute something, he began making frames for her pictures. He purchased the proper tools and found a source of artistic moldings. The combination of Marie's pictures and Paul's frames was perfect.

One day, it happened that a client of theirs was in the office and wanted to purchase one of Marie's pictures. At that moment they realized that their lives had taken a turn, and a new light had come into their lives.

Their business finally sold, and their life in retirement began. Marie painted more. She even dared to participate in a local public art exhibit. She was promptly awarded a nice little prize! This encouraged Paul to rent some space in an abandoned store and mount a short exhibit of Marie's paintings. This turned out to be a considerable success, was written up in the local paper, and many people visited the show.

Later in the year, when a regional art exhibit came along, Marie was invited to exhibit her work, and her paintings garnered yet another prize, this one more prestigious. Not to be overlooked was the fact that Paul's frames for Marie's paintings were part of the success.

And more successful exhibits in various parts of France followed.

Then something unexpected occurred. Paul had a dream of traveling on a train pulled by one of his little toy locomotives that he had sitting on that shelf in their apartment.

The next day, Paul took down that specific locomotive, which represented a historic French steam engine of Provence, and held it in his hand for a while. Not too long before, he had read a book of short stories about traveling. His mind began to develop the dream he had had the night before into a wonderful little story. He told Marie about the story.

Later that day, she came home from some errands with a wonderful blank diary book and an equally nice pen. She put them down in front of Paul and smiled at him. Paul kissed Marie, and they held hands for a moment.

By dinnertime, Paul had written out several paragraphs of his story, and he read them to Marie. She approved of them enthusiastically. Had their lives taken a new turn? Had a new light come into their lives?

When Paul finished his story about the historic train, he sent it off to some friends. Their reactions were encouraging. Soon, Paul wrote a second story and a third one.

The modern world offers many surprises. A friend of Marie and Paul put Paul's stories on a Web site, provided with a suitable title and subtitle to facilitate the stories being found through Google by people interested in travel on historic trains in France, or just by any amateur of historic trains.

Within a short time, many people from different countries—from France, from Canada, from French speakers in the United States, from the area of the former colonies of France, and from vacationers anywhere—read Paul's stories on the internet. His name became known: when typing only his name into Google, the reader was directed to his stories.

On the side, Paul began to visit and study the areas where those historic trains had circulated or were still in use. He learned all about their history and geography. Soon he was an expert in those fields of knowledge. Most importantly, he met local people in those areas, learning about their lives and, thereby, enriched his stories.

Last summer, Eva and I visited with Marie and Paul. They were perfect hosts for a delightful meal at their apartment. Before we left, I asked if I could take a photo of them. But the light in the apartment was just not bright enough.

We opened the door to their balcony, and the warm, golden rays of a wonderful afternoon sun of Provence came into their apartment.

It almost looked as if the light was then emanating from them.

We cherish this almost symbolic photo and remain fond of our friends.

Jesus of Nazareth

*

A vision—possibly offering some explanations

*

Early on Easter Sunday of this year, I had a most unusual, dreamlike vision. In my mind, I found myself standing near a village in rural Galilee as the sun had just risen and saw Jesus and a group of his followers approach. I was most vividly impressed by the great purity and radiance of Jesus—and also by his fragility. As the vision continued in my thoughts over the next few days, I participated in some of the critical phases of Jesus's wandering during his short life. I felt some of the joy, some of the anxiety, and some of the abysmal fear that pervaded his group of followers over the course of their journey. Let me describe what I saw and felt in observing Jesus and his disciples in the pursuit of their mission and in observing the plot of the adversaries closing around Jesus's existence on Earth.

*

First Picture: A Sermon on a Mount

It was after Jesus' baptism by John, and only shortly after his return from the retreat in the desert that had given him spiritual clarity about his mission. In spite of his recent asceticism, which left him very slender, Jesus appeared strong and dynamic as he walked with his followers. But what impressed me most was the purity of Jesus' expression. Only once, somewhere in a small Russian church, had I seen such purity, clarity, and goodness in the face of an adult.

Jesus had already chosen his disciples, and they were almost magnetically, truly spiritually, attracted to him. However, being naïve, they understood little of what he had on his mind. After all, they were drawn from among the fishermen and small-town people of Galilee, who were open to simple commitments, to goodness and compassion. They were not chosen from among the city intellectuals, who were too complex in their thoughts and often already set in their mental tracks, skillfully defending their own perspectives. The group was casually dressed in the Near Eastern fashion of those years and moved with ease through the rural area in the freshness of spring of that year.

This group of young men—soon augmented by more followers, including women—developed a vibrant group spirit, like a team of travelers setting out to hike through distant mountains.

Jesus's leadership was unquestioned, not because of his words, but because of his personality and his spirit. Every day was full of new experiences, excitement, and expectation. Their coming brought light and joy to the hearts of the people, and Jesus's healing power brought hope to the suffering and their families.

During this early period, the group moved almost every day, walking from village to village. As curious villagers crowded around them in dusty village centers between low houses, Jesus would speak. After he spoke, he occasionally healed the villagers who were most afflicted. For both of these reasons—the speeches and the healing—the number of his followers grew significantly. Soon, it became impractical to stop in the center of the small villages. They now stopped outside the villages, preferably where Jesus could stand on a small rise.

Late one afternoon, some time before the group reached another village, a low-level priest—we would now consider him a local rabbi—walked with Jesus and challenged him to present his teachings more clearly. Since the crowd was especially large that day and a suitable elevation for giving a speech appeared, Jesus walked up to the small mound and asked for silence. Many people sat down. Some pushed forward with the sick they wanted to present for healing. The disciples stood at the side of the mound, the priest in their midst.

Jesus began to speak with a clarity like never before, as from an internal fire. Every word, every sentence rang loud and clear. In a few simple parables, Jesus pronounced that it was not enough to follow the letter of the laws. Fulfilling the *spirit* of the laws with full intent of the heart was demanded, thereby fulfilling their moral demand. Reaching rank and wealth in this world would not count. Only those individuals who had clean hearts, who were peacemakers, who were merciful, counted before God. The meek would find reward—the ones with simple thoughts, the mourners, and those suffering from injustice. To love God and to love, forgive, and help each other should be the foremost laws for all people.

Then Jesus prayed with the people, asking God for help in life's basic struggle. He also asked for forgiveness and pronounced God as the "father in heaven."

This sermon and prayer presented moral clarity in basic terms, comfort for the suffering in the struggle of their often harsh lives, and a new image of God as a loving father.

These were the "good news," the "Ευαγγελιον," which Jesus had for the simple people of Galilee who listened and were ready to follow him.

The crowd was captivated by what it heard.

Jesus's voice can still be heard today from the Sermon on the Mount.

It still reverberates in our souls.

The priest walked away in amazement.

Second Picture: The Appearance of Authority

The priest traveled to Jerusalem during the following week. At a meeting with the High Priest of the Jerusalem temple, he described the powerful impression Jesus's Sermon on the Mount had given him. He also talked about the ever-larger group of followers around Jesus.

The high priest asked, "Was his teaching correct?" The question presented a problem. Jesus's preaching seemed not to emphasize the strictness in observing each detail in the Mosaic Law. At times, it even appeared to criticize the unlimited authority of the priestly hierarchy in interpreting the law their way and their demonstration of elite rank.

After further discussion, the High Priest decided to send another priest to distant Galilee—this time a priest from the Jerusalem temple, a man he trusted—to observe and report. That priest from Jerusalem felt honored by his assignment and took some of his students along.

Faithful servants of authority can be dangerous. They are sometimes more unbending and anxious to find error than the men of real authority who send them out. They have to prove their importance to the world by following the rules. These "organization men," as we might call them today, act as they perceive the organization expects them to act—rather than being guided by their own judgment—or by understanding, compromise, and compassion. However, their critical report, even when it concerns trivia, forces the authorities to take action.

The priest and his students arrived at a small town near Nazareth on the evening before Sabbath, planning to rest there as prescribed by Mosaic Law. The following Sabbath morning, they were surprised to see Jesus and his followers approach their town. Walking through the fields, that group could be seen reaching for some ears of wheat to feed themselves.

The priest looked at his students as if asking a test question. They shook their heads in disapproval. Harvesting, a form of work, was not allowed on a Sabbath.

Jesus and his followers entered the town. After the usual sermon, Jesus healed a suffering man, actually constituting the rendering of a service also not allowed on a Sabbath.

The priest, observing this double breach of the Sabbath rule—first the reaping of wheat, and now the healing—became so irritated that he challenged Jesus in a loud voice. Jesus deflected the challenge calmly. "Sabbath was made for man, not man for the Sabbath."

The priest walked to the synagogue in town and, shortly thereafter, departed for Jerusalem, his students in tow.

When Jesus came to the synagogue some time later, he found the doors closed. He was told that there were some renovations going on inside. One of Jesus's followers commented that the visiting priest from Jerusalem surely had something to do with locking Jesus out.

Third Picture: The Noose is Tightening, and Winter is Coming

Only two weeks later, two new groups of delegates from Jerusalem's authorities appeared to observe Jesus. One group had been sent out by the High Priest and the other by the leaders of the Pharisees. They could be easily recognized by their hats, their manner of dress, and their Jerusalem accent.

From that point on, Jesus could seldom preach a sermon without some observers being present. When one of Jesus's disciples saw them approach, he notified the others, and warned Jesus to be on guard.

It soon became a war of nerves. These "observers" stood silently, sometimes taking notes. However, when Jesus seemed to have the most success with his audience, they asked loud, disturbing questions.

Initially, Jesus deflected the questions posed by these gadflies. But as the questions turned more critical, he became impatient with them. After that, he preached about the fallibility of priests, Pharisees, and scribes.

Jesus's followers were well aware of the growing controversy. As time went on, there was hardly a town or village where Jesus was allowed to enter the synagogues. Sometimes, he was asked to remain outside the settlements.

Jesus's followers stood ever closer around their master. Their faces became somber. At one point, Jesus asked them whether they still believed in him. Their responses were clear expressions of their commitment, but still, their hearts were heavy.

Finally, winter came upon them, with its endless cold rain and sometimes snow on the mountaintops. It became difficult, sometimes impossible for Jesus's large group—twelve disciples, some women, and some other followers—to find accommodation and food in the villages and small towns. They were wet, hungry, and freezing.

Life became harsh.

At one point, Jesus divided the group, instructing his disciples to go out by themselves, only two in each group, and continue their mission, preaching and healing wherever they went. Some returned to their villages, families, and friends for the winter.

Fourth Picture: The Vision on the Mountain

Winter finally came to an end. But even before Jesus could call his dispersed disciples back together, the first critical observers from Jerusalem reappeared.

At this point, Jesus went up to a high mountain to seek spiritual counsel.

From the time of that spiritual encounter on the mountain on, Jesus knew that he could not continue in Galilee alone and that he had to go directly to Jerusalem to confront the powers arrayed against him, face to face. The approaching spring celebrations of Passover in Jerusalem would be the time to implement this decision.

Fifth Picture: Spring and the Last Days in Jerusalem

From this time on, Jesus's sermons acquired new force, clarity, and determination. Not glory in this life, but later reward in Heaven should be expected by all good people. At the same time, Jesus began to warn Jerusalem of impending danger, should it continue on its present path.

Jesus's disciples had all returned to be around him again, even the one who appeared to have had a rather good time during winter. There are always some weak or unscrupulous followers following great leaders, and great leaders seem to tolerate them. However, some of these followers are more dangerous than others, and some are less trustworthy than others.

One in particular, Judas, had relatives and friends among the priests. They had entertained him during winter in order to learn more about his master's teachings. He had tried to present a compromise approach while doing some fundraising for Jesus's group, something he was quite good at.

Then came the time for Jesus and his group to begin their one hundred kilometer pilgrimage to Jerusalem for Passover. There was heavy traffic on the way from Galilee to Jerusalem as the high holidays approached. Many travelers to the Passover celebrations knew Jesus and welcomed him, as their great preacher and healer and one of their people from the North. Jesus's reputation, possibly amplified by the Galileans, preceded him to Jerusalem.

When Jesus arrived in Jerusalem, the shining city with its great temple and urbane crowds was ready for him. Clothing was spread in his way in the hope that the transient contact with Jesus would bring blessings to the owners. People who could not spare clothing spread branches of trees, palm fronds, on the road. The jubilation of the multitude fed on itself in this glorious moment of Jesus's triumphal entry into Jerusalem.

Jesus remained somber, however. He knew that his decisive battle was approaching and that the end required his sacrifice. There was no return, no compromise; but he did not fear it.

On this last day, Jesus was not withdrawn. When he found the merchants and money changers in the court of the great temple precinct, he took action. He did not even talk to the priests about his concerns about the purity of the House of God. He just drove the merchants and money changers out in a fury, acting as the supreme judge and leader of the people.

Just as the Sermon on the Mount was the zenith of Jesus's spiritual impact on the world, so this day and following dinner meal with his disciples in Jerusalem was the zenith of his forceful actions in the world. This was the day of ultimate strength, clarity of purpose, and leadership, finally turning into the conclusion of his mission.

The day came to an end. Jesus knew what would follow. The priests had to act or their world would crumble.

At the dinner, Jesus spoke clearly about his coming sacrifice. He symbolized his sacrifice with the partaking of wine and bread, appealing to his disciples to always remember his mission. Then he turned toward Judas.

Judas may have been a double agent from the winter months on, continuing to contact his friends among the priests while remaining a disciple of Jesus. He may have been the first of Jesus's followers to know, that day in Jerusalem, that Jesus's fate had been sealed. He may even have warned Jesus just before the Passover dinner. This might have opened Jesus's eyes that Judas could not be trusted, as some of his other disciples might have already hinted for some time before.

Jesus suddenly addressed Judas as a traitor and dismissed him.

While Judas rushed out in anger toward full cooperation with the priests, Jesus departed for his last night with his closest followers and for his final prayer to his God and master in the garden of Gethsemane.

The harshness of the end of his mission that had started so radiantly and the approach of his painful death in mental loneliness lay before him.

The council of the priestly authorities and the leaders of the Pharisees had to come to a conclusion, in view of the crowds' jubilation around Jesus and, mainly, in view of Jesus's authoritative action in clearing the temple, the seat and pillar of their exclusive power.

The council was divided, as most councils are. One member of the council suggested that if Jesus was of God, nothing could be done against him. However, if he was not of God, time would take care of him, as it had done of other false prophets not long before.

The council of the priests was controlled by an archconservative. The vote was to kill Jesus immediately, creating "facts on the ground," before the always unpredictable masses of people congregated to begin the Passover celebrations and before the crowd of Galilean followers had a chance to regroup.

With the arrival of Judas and the police in the garden of Gethsemane, the establishment began to exterminate its perceived subverter, step by step, through interrogation, false witnesses, torture, condemnation, and quick execution.

How horrible these last hours of his life must have been for Jesus.

Nobody came out in support of Jesus in those last hours.

None of the crowd that had welcomed him jubilantly the day before.

What must have been on Jesus's mind when none of those spoke up to whose aid he had come and for whose sake he had brought his message of mercy and peace, his vision of respecting the meek and the peacemakers, and his demand that they help those who suffered from injustice?

His own disciples had fled, and one had even denied him.

For whom was Jesus going to sacrifice himself?

The reports about Jesus's last moments differ. One speaks of an ending in great despair. Another tells us of Jesus looking up to God and passing away in great peace, saying, "My work is done."

Postscript: The Persecutions of the Early Christians and Paulus

The Galileans returned to the north. Jesus's immediate followers stayed in Jerusalem, close to their executed master's grave, going "underground" to evade persecution. The crowds in Jerusalem, which had cheered Jesus only a few days earlier, had turned around or acted in submission and passivity, as all crowds do. The Christ's teachings were finished, or so it seemed.

Then came the apparitions of Jesus to his followers: the ascension phenomenon and, most dramatically, Pentecost. This overwhelming spiritual experience gave Jesus's followers renewed strength. Groups of committed "Christians" began to form.

It did not take long for the authorities to hear about Jesus's resurrection and the reappearance of Jesus's followers—the Christians. One of Jesus's priestly judges had predicted, "If (Jesus) was not of God, time would take care of him." But time had not taken care of Jesus's teachings or the Christians. Was God with them, after all? Their numbers grew. It became necessary to act. The persecutions set in. The groups dispersed and then found new followers in distant cities.

The brash and ambitious Saulus made himself a name as an exterminator of Jesus's adherents—but only of those who did not strictly submit to Judaic Laws and priestly authority. After cleaning up Jerusalem, he traveled to Damascus, which was many days of travel away. Then the unexplainable occurred: Saulus became Paulus, a most ardent Christian.

Paulus gave Jesus's teachings a new turn. From now on, his teachings were presented on the level of a coherent theology and philosophy, as influenced by Greek thought. Sin and redemption, faith in Christ, and the goal of reaching heaven moved into the foreground, sometimes at the expense of the basic teachings of the Sermon on that Mount. The group of followers, previously restricted to Jews, was opened up to the people of all nations. The dramatic growth of Christianity away from Judaism, which Jesus had cared for most, began.

A small group in Jerusalem attempted to restrain Paulus (or Paul, as he is known to us)—to no avail.

Then, the hierarchy of priests in Jerusalem was swept away in the destruction of that splendid city by the Romans. Only a few Pharisees escaped to become the rabbis of Jewish centers in the Diaspora.

The original groups of Christians dispersed throughout the Roman Empire. Those who had stayed in Jerusalem remained together and migrated to what later became Arabia. They were later known by Muhammad and, thereby, influenced the origin of the teachings of Islam.

The Roman Christians and followers of Paul became dominant in the West, forming and participating in Europe's triumph in the world—all too often failing to follow the teachings of their master about humility, a clean heart, peacemaking, and being merciful; all too often overlooking the meek, those with simple thoughts, the mourners, and those suffering from injustice.

The world went its way toward modernity, remembering Christ in one basic symbol, not one related to his light-filled mission and essential ethical teaching of the first days, not related to his most forceful action of later days, but to his darkest moment on the cross.

What if Rome had not become Christian? What course would the Western world have taken through history? Where would our civilization stand in regard to ethics and other social thought? Would there have been welfare, a Red Cross, all the charitable work in the world, and foreign assistance among nations? Shouldn't we be glad to live in our civilization as it is now? Do we gladly remember Jesus for his mission and its effect?

The Moment of Light that Came and Went

*

A transcendental vision—
three weeks after September 11, 2001

*

As the world entered into this horribly dark phase of violence, it just so happened that Moses, Jesus, and Mohammed met on a cloud in Paradise. They sat down with somber faces and began to talk.

"How can Muslims commit such atrocities?" said Mohammed.

"How can Christians let the world slide into such a predicament?" said Jesus.

"What have the Jews done with their vision of God, with the Holy Land entrusted to them?" said Moses.

They exchanged more thoughts.

"What have the spiritual leaders of our religions done to guide people in the modern world?"

"Did we not leave clear instructions to our followers?"

"How can we justify the consequences of our teachings before our common God?"

The three men went to God and asked to be allowed to return to Earth to correct the situation, to give clear guidance to the people and stern instructions to the spiritual leaders of their respective religions. God allowed them to go down, but only for one day.

On the given day—I wish it could be tomorrow—they decided to go down together. They agreed to appear in Jerusalem together. They decided to visit three locations: in front of the Wailing Wall, on the Temple Mount next to the great mosque, and in front of the Church of the Sepulcher.

Their appearances brought wonder to Jerusalem. Celestial light and cosmic harmonies filled the air. As evidence of the divine nature of their coming, all three together appeared at the three chosen locations within Jerusalem at the same time, but Moses spoke at the Western Wall, Jesus at the Church of the Sepulcher, and Mohammed at the mosque on the Temple Mount. Every individual in the quickly accumulating large crowds of people heard the messenger speak in his own native tongue. Other wonders were done—sick people were cured, obsessed were freed of bad spirits, and the three heavenly personalities levitated.

What were their messages?

"How could you forget the greatness of God?" Moses said to the people gathered. "He was your forceful leader in the early years, when you had to establish yourselves as a nation in a strange land. He gave you the Ten Commandments for civilized life when you settled down. He taught you to 'love your neighbor as yourself' as you walked on into the future. You were the chosen people to guide all mankind. How could you settle down and find satisfaction in formally observing more than six hundred laws of conduct, while not being a blessing to your own neighbors? How could you be blessed with the greatest mental gifts and wealth among all nations, and not set an example in resolving the problems of tribal neighborly strife as affects so many other regions on Earth? God created the whole world. All people are his children— your brothers and sisters. As his chosen people, you are expected to lead toward a world where your neighbors can also live a fulfilled life. Did you not contribute to setting the present fire? Wake up to your responsibility. Act now as if tomorrow were the day of reckoning."

"Did you forget the liberating thoughts I gave you: to be meek, merciful, pure in heart, and peacemakers?" said Jesus. "How could you forget the poorest of the poor among the nations? How could you give support to the mighty who suppress the poor? You gave them weapons and money, and you taught them the skills to do what they do. You were given the greatest civilization and insight of all people in history. Did you apply enough of your knowledge and means for the betterment of this fragile world, rather than for your own well-being?

What should the world that God has offered to you be like? What did each one of you do in your little or large circle of life to let a better world appear? Much will be expected from the one to whom much was given. Wake up to your responsibility. Act now as if tomorrow were the day of reckoning!"

"Have you forgotten that an angel revealed to me a God of mercy and compassion, as every Surah states at its beginning?" said Mohammed. "What God asks of you is first, and only, a pious and moral life. God abhors the killing of the innocent. The God of the Jews, of the Christians, and of you is the same God, because there is only one God. God has created all mankind: you, the Jews, the Christians, and all others, too. If you believe in our God as revealed to me, you must live a more pious and more moral life. Be an example to the infidel. You must be merciful and compassionate. Yes, in the Second Surah, 192nd verse, I directed you to kill those who fight against you when they are the unprovoked aggressors in taking your freedom or land. But in the same Surah, 191st verse, I directed you not to transgress limits. Clearly, you cannot commit atrocities against the innocent. Those days of my revelations were the violent days of human society. I was the last to present divine revelation to you. This did not mean that human society stopped evolving, as it has evolved from the earliest time on. Wake up to the modern world. Show the world that piety and morality can be a guide toward a better world without hatred and violence, but a world with mercy and compassion. Wake up to your responsibility as the true believers in our common God. Act now as if tomorrow were the day of reckoning!"

When all this was heard, the Jews danced for joy, the Christians fell on their knees, and the Muslims prayed toward Mecca. Then they all embraced each other and became one people in their diversity under one God.

They started building one common temple on the Mount to the common God.

The holy personalities re-ascended toward heaven in joy. They had been understood.

The next day, the supreme mullahs, the greatest of the rabbis, the Pope and all cardinals met in their respective sanctuaries for council. They questioned some exuberant witnesses. They analyzed the theological content of what was reported to them. They calculated the consequences for their systems of dogma and their hierarchical positions.

After a week, the conclusions came out. The words that were heard in Jerusalem contained nothing new. Each religion's theological dogma had no need to be changed. The faithful of all three religious directions were admonished to be even more obedient to the old teachings. Furthermore, the short apparition in Jerusalem to only a few people was judged to be of doubtful veracity.

More settlements were expanded in the occupied territories, the fight against terrorism continued, and mullahs continued preaching for a Holy War against the infidel. A common meeting of the spiritual leaders and a common declaration to address the grave crisis of the world did not occur.

The three divine personalities met on the cloud in Paradise once more. For the first time in history, the three together cried in common anguish.

The world had not changed … unless we all change—together; now—as if tomorrow were the day of reckoning!

*

But then, on January 24, 2002, Pope John Paul II actually convened a meeting of leading representatives of the different confessions at Assisi, Italy, to address the problems of violence and terrorism in the world.

A declaration resulted, named the Assisi Decalogue for Peace, presenting ten basic commitments for peace.

The commitments propose peaceful solutions to all conflicts, but they do not address the religious fundamentalism on all sides, military countermeasures that are accepted as necessary against unending large-scale terrorism, military occupation, the establishment of settlements in occupied territories, the total attrition of the livelihood of whole populations, the spirals of mutual revenge, and the acts of desperation.

The Assisi Decalogue for Peace was sent to many heads of state and government and to the media. The report about the Assisi meeting and the resulting declaration appeared in many newspapers at that time.

After that, there was no follow-up, and it was quickly forgotten.

The Death of the Taliban Fighter

*

A beautiful vision turns into darkness

*

Abdul had grown up as the fourth child of a tailor in Kunduz, a small town in northeastern Afghanistan. He was somewhat small and lightly built, compared to his brothers, and of a more serious mind.

One evening, his mother took the children out of the house to see the stars in the night. She sang a sweet little melody. In the song, she named the brightest of the twinkling stars and spoke about Allah who lived above them. Little Abdul thought he could see Allah's friendly face in the darkness and felt very happy. Since that night, Abdul wanted to learn all he could about the world around him, the names of all the stars and also of all the plants and animals, and where they lived. Instead of running around in the streets with the other boys, he enjoyed sitting next to his father, learning to read and write.

The Taliban were in control of the city, business was slow, and there was not enough money in the family to send Abdul to school. But school was what he longed for most. One day, an uncle came to visit. He had done well with a little business across the mountains in Pakistan, on the Karakorum Highway that led down from China along the upper Indus valley and past the enormous Nanga Parbat Mountain to Islamabad and Rawalpindi. This uncle was impressed by Abdul's learning and proposed that he attend a school run by a mullah in the uncle's vicinity. The uncle would graciously pay for the schooling expenses for the best son of his nicest brother.

The school, it turned out, was actually a madrasa, where a village mullah made a living for himself and his family by boarding some thirty-five boys in Spartan accommodations while teaching them all he knew about the Koran, however much or little that was. At first, Abdul was disappointed that he didn't learn anything about the stars, plants, and animals. But then he discovered another world, the world of the Koran, the teaching of the right course through life that would give him access to paradise, and he learned about so many old stories of Allah's help to people in the historic past. Would Allah help his family, too, one day?

The mullah treated his students well. At the end of Ramadan, the mullah's wife brought them some of the sweet pastries that she always baked for the mullah, and the students could smell the wonderful aroma of the roast she was preparing. After all, when the mullah ate well, he was less stern in his teaching, as when he described paradise.

Then the fighting in Afghanistan began with some American bombings around distant Mazar i Sharif. The Taliban called for more volunteers for their jihad. Abdul had just turned seventeen and thought about joining the holy war against the infidel. The mullah wanted to make a name for the holiness of his madrasa by sending some volunteers. Some of his students were village boys of little inclination for learning, who might possibly have good fighting skills and who were also not paying much tuition to the mullah.

The better students were mostly the sons or nephews of merchants who paid full tuition and brought gifts. Abdul belonged to the latter. The mullah didn't want to let him go, but Abdul insisted. It was Ramadan again, and on the evening before his departure, the mullah brought him some extra food before he sat down with his family for the usual feast. The mullah felt good about sending twelve of his students, even Abdul, the serious one, to the Taliban.

The group of young volunteers left during the night, in order to not be discovered by the Pakistani border police or by the assumed enemy. As the first light of morning appeared, they had already crossed the pass into Afghanistan and walked down into a beautiful valley, with trees along the course of a small river, dense bushes, and occasional small, well-tended fields. Abdul felt like he was coming home.

A group of armed men stopped the group of youngsters. As they learned that the young men were volunteers, they became friendly. Only one of them was different, the leader of the armed group. They were told he was an al Qaeda fighter. He was arrogant and stern, as if he was better than the rest of them. He ordered the volunteers to stop talking and to carry heavy loads of supplies that had just been delivered from Pakistan. There wouldn't be any food until the evening.

Several days of marching later, they arrived in Kunduz. Abdul's parents had fled. All his former friends had been drafted by the Taliban, the wilder ones by al Qaeda. The young volunteers were taught how to use guns and were ordered to stay in stables now serving as barracks. Was that the holy war leading to paradise?

Then the American bombing of Kunduz started. At first, the group of volunteers heard some explosions in the far distance during the night. Hours later, some wounded fighters were brought in.

Every night, the explosions came closer and turned louder. Upon one of the worst of the explosions, the building began to rattle and the air was filled with dust. They had received very little food lately and only bad water. Some of the wounded men were brought into their compound—some had only shrapnel holes through their bodies, others had parts of their limbs torn away—crying loudly, staying silent, or just whimpering in pain. Nobody dared to go out during the night any longer, and their room became a stinky mess. They prayed for many hours through the night, but some just stared into the darkness. They knew that they would not escape this horror.

The next night, the bombing started early, right after sunset. Abdul thought of the mullah who would now be sitting down with his family for dinner. A bomb hit the side of their building. The explosion was deafening. Roof beams fell on the volunteers and the wounded soldiers. Some were killed.

Suddenly, Abdul was filled with enormous rage against the mullah. He thought he saw him standing there. He took his rifle and fired wildly at what he saw.

An older, wounded soldier next to him quietly put a hand on his arm and said, "Allah is merciful and compassionate."

With the next bomb explosion, Abdul heard two distinct metallic sounds. Were they the first notes of that melody his mother had once sung?

Abdul got up and walked out into the night.

He looked up at the bright stars, but he couldn't see Allah's face above them in the empty darkness.

He didn't even hear the whistling of the bomb that came down to tear him apart.

... and Then, the Sounds of an Aria!

*

Greetings to a future reader

*

We drove through heavy midday traffic in town and listened to the radio—and then, unexpectedly, there came the sounds of an aria as wonderful as only Italian composers and Mozart had created. The words were insignificant, but the sounds of the harmonies gave them meaning. I sensed joy, a bit of sadness, some light, and a resonance of my soul—if "soul" still exists in our modern world. There, they had composed this music some 150 years ago, possibly for a rich sponsor, had put the best of their sensitivity into those melodies, and created a gift for us in our time, in this remote town, far from their lives. If only we, too, could send some beautiful, comforting messages to a future world, rather than always struggle through daily insignificance. What would we want to communicate? Possibly some simple images of our time that have been overlooked by the media and the fashionable.

*

Are there sounds of idealism, sadness, love, hope to communicate from our lives?

Some adults sat around in a group and talked about their children, who had left college some years ago and were supposed to be successful in their own lives.

There was the mother of two children. Those children had joined a charitable organization out of idealism right after college and had moved to an underdeveloped country to help the poor. Now, they had returned and were having trouble finding jobs to build their own lives and start their own families. They had given the so-called "best years of their lives" for others. Who would help them now? If only someone could help them. But trust; they will succeed.

The other mother had a daughter who had studied art and had supported her boyfriend while he finished his studies. Once the boy had finished his studies, their friendship broke up. The pursuit of art had not yielded very much for that daughter either. Instead, she thought about opening a restaurant. Was that the outcome of all her youthful idealism and self-sacrifice in this world? If only she would find some light and happiness in her life. But the boy still loves her. Will they untangle the course of their lives and be married after all?

There was the old couple who still had to care for their much older parents who were not always modest in their expectations of care. What remained of a fulfilling life for them? Maybe just one quiet evening, just for the two of them to spend together in harmony?

Do not let the light of your life be extinguished. Do not burn out. You have to be practical in this unforgiving world—where you need income for a life of freedom and dignity; where you have to set limits; but where human joy and warmth still gives deeper meaning to life.

Do not give up in your search for friendship and love, which support real life and make it tolerable. Just think that possibly tomorrow, possibly next year, but maybe only in five years, the fortunate change will occur. Life can last long and be full of surprises.

I know a couple that didn't find each other until they were fifty. I knew a prisoner of war who only gained freedom after eleven years, but then lived the happiest years of his life with his wife who had waited for him. I know several young people, who, for some time, were quite unhappy and without success at their jobs, until the big opportunity came, which they were able to perceive and grasp. Or they were lonely until they found the right partners for their lives, and they now enjoy lives full of light and meaning.

One of them, warmhearted as he is, returns his late-found joy of life by contributing to others.

Can you not look beyond yourself to see the world in its varied dimensions? The world does offer joy. The view of some beautiful scenery, of a nice garden, or of just a few flowers is enough to experience joy. Sometimes it is enough to observe a busy street in a large city, to see some happy young people or some interesting older ones.

Just go out into life, into this colorful world. Participate in the joy of life. See the golden light of the morning, the brightness of noon, the mildness of evening.

Look at the clouds and feel the refreshing rain. You experience more joy if you participate creatively.

Somebody received much help in his younger years. The helpers did not accept any compensation. Much later, this person met some young people who needed help to fix their car for their big journey. That person helped and did not accept compensation either. He asked only that the help be passed on sometime, somewhere, to somebody else. The young people drove off happily into the world, waving back as they departed. Where may this chain of helping be moving along now?

An old man checked his mailbox every day, waiting for a letter that never arrived. One day, he sat down in his garden. A small bird arrived and sang a beautiful song. The old man did not wait for the letter any longer, but he watched as the little bird found a partner, built a nest, and raised some chicks, which then fluttered happily out into their world. In winter, the old man provided some food to the birds, and waited for the next nests to be built in spring. Life has its own way of moving merrily on, but it follows its own path. Keep your eyes open for life.

And how about happiness, even exuberance?

A grandfather and grandchild were expected to go for a walk. The day was sunny and warm. The flowers bloomed in the verdant gardens, and the trees provided refreshing shade. The little granddaughter did not like to walk. She preferred skipping along. So she asked her grandpa, "Can you skip, too?"

"Let's see if we can," he said. "Look here!" And they both skipped happily along: forward with one foot, skip, forward with the other foot, skip. You could compose a little exuberant melody for that. They skipped along for the whole length of the block. Then they stopped to rest because grandpa was a bit out of breath, and they laughed and laughed for a while.

Can arias be noble?

Where is there still anything noble in our modern world? Is it not noble to forget selfishness for once? Is it not noble to have the good and beautiful in mind?

Thus, a child may do something noble, as an adult, or a politician, or a hero.

You can do something noble, now, by touching somebody else's life and giving that person joy thereby.

Call somebody up, without any reason. Or send an e-mail, as is so easily done in our days—with just a few clicks.

I received the answer to one of my e-mails this morning. Actually, my e-mail had been rather simple. The answer was quite simple, too, but it came from the heart. Someone had understood me and had felt joy. And now, I feel joy, too. It was like a nice sound in the course of life—for just a moment—that still resonates.

This story is quite simple, too, but it also came from the heart.

Did it leave a sound? Did it possibly resonate for a moment? Was it the sound of love, a bit of sadness, hope, some light, even exuberance— the resonance of a long life?

Accept it as a gift of the moment. Then, sing your own aria.

Sing the song of your life, of warm love, of a little sadness, and of much joy— maybe you'll also sing of a moment of exuberance.

Send it to somebody else.

Or save it somewhere, where a hundred years from now somebody else can find it and feel some joy.

Troy

The light and the darkness of a troubled life
*

What gives light to an image? The light in an image is given by the bright areas that you perceive and that remain in your mind and memory, sometimes augmented in their effect by the shadows, unless the shadows are very dark, disturbing, and prevalent. I want to believe in the positive side of my fellow human beings. I saw and still remember the light in Troy's troubled life—and wish that the darkness could still be lifted. What else would I have felt or done if he had really been one of my brothers?

*

I met Troy when I did some volunteer work in the low-income section of a formerly industrial and now impoverished city of America. It could have been in any such part of a city anywhere in the world. I met Troy in the black section of town, where many women had been abandoned by their husbands and raised a number of children as single mothers on welfare, but it could have been in a white part of a declining mining town in Appalachia, or anywhere else in the world. Several houses were abandoned and boarded up. Most houses looked in disrepair. Once in a while, a family was able to pull itself courageously together, stay together, keep their house in good shape, and raise decent children with a bright future.

Most outstanding in that neighborhood was a house on a side street. It was just a simple two-story row house next to a vacant and abandoned lot. The house was covered with gray stucco. A few steps led up to the entrance, and a narrow window was on each side. But remarkable about the house was that it featured a row of very beautiful flower pots in full bloom lined up on either side of the entrance steps.

"Who lives there?" I inquired of people passing by.

"Oh, that's just Troy—a little disturbed. You know what I mean!"

No, I did not know what was meant. Upon further inquiry, I only learned that Troy was an elderly black man, without a job, who occasionally cleaned the street to the right and left of his house, helped anybody who needed a hand and lived on welfare on account of a mental problem or some mental weakness.

One day, I stopped in front of Troy's house as I was driving by with my wife. Troy stood in front of all his flowers. He was an elderly man, tall and rather thin, with graying, short-cropped hair, and a dark-black complexion.

I rolled down my window and said, "Wonderful, your flowers there!"

Troy's eyes lit up. He immediately grabbed one of the flower pots and walked over. He presented the flowers to my wife, with a radiant, warm smile that showed his white teeth, saying "Please share in my joy of flowers."

Winter passed, and the next spring arrived. When I drove through that area again, I noticed something on the formerly vacant and totally abandoned lot right close to Troy's house. Somebody had established a small patch of nicely arranged stones in its middle. In the center, a small white statue of the Virgin Mary stood on an artful wooden frame, with an American flag on each side. As soon as I could, I visited Troy to inquire.

Yes, it was he who had arranged that display. He had found an old article about the appearance of the Madonna of Fatima and had been so touched by this appearance many years ago in Portugal that he felt like building a memorial for that Madonna on that empty lot next to his house. Was he hoping for her blessings for this blighted part of the world? The rough youngsters of the neighborhood took to disturbing the display at night. So Troy had to take not only the flags but also the statue of the Madonna into his house every evening and put them up again the next morning.

A few days later, I happened to drive by a nursery and saw that geraniums were for sale. I bought more than a dozen red, pink, and white ones and brought them to Troy, who accepted them joyfully with his radiant and warm smile and, this time, with an embrace. He would happily use the flowers to further decorate that memorial.

We had become friends. I stopped many times at Troy's house. He usually rushed out to greet me most cordially with his big smile, occasionally even with an embrace. We then talked for a while before I had to move on to pursue my assigned tasks in town. In his simple way of life, Troy reminded me of the Sermon on the Mount—blessed are the meek, blessed are those who are simple of mind, blessed are those with a clean heart—or of Jesus's praise of the children.

In the course of these meetings, Troy told me about his life.

Troy was born in poverty sixty-six years earlier as the son of a black farm laborer in Louisiana. Troy must have had a good father, one who later took him along as a small boy to Newark, New Jersey, where his father had found better work. The new boss, a wealthy white landowner, must have been a good man, too. He invited little Troy to play with his children. Even more, he scratched their children's and Troy's hands just a little and had them touch each other—as in the stories of old—and declared them "blood brothers."

Troy did not take to school very well. Instead, he became an excellent and intelligent farm worker. He was promoted to supervisor of the Hispanic migrant workers who showed up for a few months every year at harvest time.

Later, a lawyer friend of Troy's boss noticed Troy's intelligence and offered him a job in his office, mainly carrying documents to or from the courthouse and to or from other lawyers. The lawyer also taught Troy the fundamentals of contract and trial work. Troy later told me that he participated in many trials and that his party always won.

I was also led to believe that Troy joined a local black chapter of the Masons or a similar men's association, which held their meetings in an upstairs room above a local bar. When I went to look for it, the designated building with its bar was in disrepair and appeared to be abandoned. One day, though, I noticed some well-dressed elderly black men walk in through a back door leading to the upper floor. Did the Masons still meet there?

One day, Troy continued by telling me—with a very serious, almost scared face that I had never seen on him before—how he once woke up and "heard the silence of death" all around him. What a remarkable expression! He told me that he was so scared that he stayed home all day. In the evening, as he became hungry, he finally went out to get some food. This took him past that bar below the Mason's meeting place.

Had he possibly wanted to stop in at the bar? For the moment, he told me, he had stayed on the other side of the street. He had been in that bar some time back and an especially rough drinker had given him a bad time for his fancy dress and sophisticated way of speaking. When he left the bar in disgust that day, the ruffian had followed him, and, in the middle of the street, had beaten him up badly. The other bar customers had just looked on without helping him or calling for help. Later, a friend of Troy's had slipped a pistol into Troy's coat pocket, meant to serve as defense in case of future life-threatening trouble—or so Troy told me.

This evening now, as Troy was passing the bar, that same ruffian just happened to emerge from its door. Seeing Troy passing by on the other side of the street, he ran over, shouting, "This time I will really get you!"

Troy continued by telling me that he became so scared that he instinctively reached for the gun in his pocket. A single shot was fired. The bullet killed the ruffian instantly.

This time, the other bar customers reacted differently, immediately calling the police. Troy ended up in jail for ten years, so he reported to me.

After his release many years ago, he lived quietly in his house with his flowers, a model citizen and good neighbor, as it appeared to me. Yet, he was kept at a distance by his neighbors.

Only once did I see Troy get angry, all of a sudden, when some visitor had interrupted him for a second time while he was talking to me. During that moment, Troy became a different man. His face distorted in bitterness, and sharp words came out of his mouth, but just for a moment. Then he became calm again and was his own friendly self.

I have sometimes noted this phenomenon of sudden rage in meek people. You better beware. They have to know how to defend themselves when cornered in an often cruel world. But, in the long run, their momentary rage may actually hurt them.

A few months after I heard Troy's life story, a murder occurred in that same vicinity. The corpse was found in the abandoned bar under the Mason's former meeting place. To my dismay, I learned that Troy had been picked up by the police.

Through very unlikely circumstances, I happened to meet the lawyer who had helped Troy on earlier occasions. I learned a different story. I began to feel like I was reading one of those Scott Fitzgerald stories that start in happy, harmonious settings and then fall apart, chapter by chapter, until they end in darkness.

I learned that the first shadow had fallen on Troy's life in his younger years, when he worked as the supervisor of migrant workers. Troy had developed a hot temper at that time. There was a nasty incident in which Troy hurt a farm laborer. But a lawyer friend pulled Troy out of that one.

A few other incidents of hot temper must have occurred along the way. But then, there was the report of an incident with a group of men standing in front of a bar. A shot was fired and another man was killed. Troy was accused of having fired that shot. But his lawyer was able to convince the jury that there was no unequivocal proof that it was actually Troy who had fired that shot, and he went free once more.

Next, it was rumored that Troy worked for a while as a police informer in his part of town. There was a scandal involving improper payments by the police to the informers in return for kickbacks. Troy became implicated and ended up with a multiyear prison sentence—if my information is correct—because the story sounds different, depending on who is telling it.

After his release from prison, Troy returned to his wife and two sons. Yes, it turned out that Troy had been living for a few years with a woman in a common law marriage. One of the sons was from his wife's earlier partner; the second may have been his own, or so Troy believed.

One evening, when sitting on their porch, Troy told me, he and his wife had observed a break-in down the street. They reported it to the police and that fact was reported in the local newspaper. Shortly thereafter, when Troy was out for a moment to have a drink at a bar, a car pulled up to his house, driven by the same men who had done the break-in, so Troy reported. At that time, Troy's wife was standing at the fence of their house. The men drove their car into Troy's wife, pressing her hard against the fence. They left before any witnesses could appear. Troy's wife died shortly thereafter in the hospital, but not without having declared Troy not guilty in this accident. The police investigation brought no further evidence, and Troy was not accused—nor were the drivers of the car.

Ten years later, when the murder just recently occurred in the area where Troy lived, some way or other, Troy's name appeared in the papers. To every-body's surprise, his older son—or rather his stepson—long departed from home, showed up once more. He brought new accusations against Troy, accusing him of murdering his mother ten years earlier. He claimed that when Troy came back from time in prison, he accused his wife of infidelity during his absence. One day, in a fit of renewed rage, he was accused of having beaten his wife to death while his stepson, a very young boy at that time, watched from the top of the stairs. Other people also stepped forward to testify against Troy.

That was the reason why Troy had been arrested; there is no statute of limitations for murder.

Until then, I had only known Troy as a model citizen in that neighborhood and as a cordial human being with a ready smile. We had become friends. How could I drop him based on an accusation that could prove to be wrong? Should he not be considered innocent until proven guilty?

It took me some time to locate Troy in one of the state prisons called the "workhouse." It took me even more time to have him put me on his visitor's list. This is a protective measure, keeping the inmates safe from undesirable visitors.

Finally, I drove out to the workhouse, which was a few miles up the river, where rows of steep wooded hills extend on each side. I remember distinctly how, by coincidence—as in a spooky story—it was a cloudy, dark day of fall, and a group of black birds, vultures or crows, circled overhead. Up on the hill, the low buildings of the workhouse stood, surrounded by high chain-link fences topped with razor wire.

I had to go through several fences, sign in, and wait with the other visitors— only about twenty or thirty of them—why not more for the hundreds of prisoners? Most of the visitors were black, some Hispanic, but only a few working-class white. What is wrong with our society that causes this imbalance? Where is the guilt, with the prisoners or with the system?

Some of the visitors were older—parents of the inmates? Some were mid-dle-age—the spouses? Some females were in their late teens or early twenties— sweethearts? And there were some children being dragged along.

After about half an hour, we were allowed in, walking past a spacious gym— working out and bodybuilding is a big pastime of inmates—and, five or six of the visitors at a time were lined up on stools in front of as many windows. On the other side of each window was another stool in another room. After a while, the inmates were guided into the room on the other side of the windows by guards, recognizing their respective visitors with joy or indifference. The sound of the conversation had to pass through narrow slits below the windows. It became very loud as everybody tried to communicate with his partner. We all bent down to the sound slits, and so did the inmates. In this curved position, just seeing the back of the partner on the other side, we passed a long time. What can you really talk about in such a situation?

Troy, still with his smile, yet some sadness in his expression, reiterated his innocence. He declared as false the testimonies of his stepson and the other witnesses. His stepson had been involved in some drug dealings, and the other witnesses had their own criminal cases pending. He indicated that he would send me some documents to prove it.

I visited Troy regularly for several months. By all I could learn, I was the only visitor to ever come to talk and listen to him. Then he was transferred to the state's central high-security prison. Again, it took some time to get on Troy's visitor list. Again, a certain trip by car to the prison, but then a bigger parking lot, a much bigger building, high walls instead of fences, more thorough sign-in and inspection procedures by the numerous, very correct guards. Then a first entry, but only into a very narrow courtyard surrounded by thirty-foot-high dark-gray concrete walls and a watch tower, and then through a tall, steel gate and some fences to a large building.

Inside that central building was a large gym-like, brightly lit hall with many chairs and some tables; there was even a children's section with some plastic toys. After a while, the inmates filed in. We were about a hundred visitors, and about seventy inmates came—most (but not all) convicted for repeat drug-related crimes—so I was told—worthy to be locked away to protect society. Why were there not more visitors for the three thousand inmates in that prison?

I observed one elderly father as he visited with his rough-looking and not very responsive son every time I was there. One woman told me that she had been coming every Saturday for many years to see a family member. But how about all the other inmates? And did anyone ever think of the sacrifice and suffering of the visitors?

Pairs and family groups were quickly united and set in separate areas. We had hours to talk—almost too long, it seemed to me.

On one wall was an exhibit of paintings created by the inmates. They were absolutely astounding. Of course there was a portrait of Martin Luther King Jr. and there were paintings of some beautiful young maidens. But there were also many paintings of wonderful flowers and dreamlike scenery in some distant country of freedom, some representing Africa.

On the other side of that hall was an enclosure where you could get sandwiches and soft drinks from dispensing machines. I walked to the water fountain. A middle-aged Puerto Rican fetched me a cup and offered it with a smile. After my second visit, he and I began to talk. At age twenty, he had a bar fight, and his adversary died in the fight. Since he had once muttered "one day I will kill that guy," it counted as premeditated murder. He was sentenced to thirty years.

Twenty long years had passed. In ten years, at age fifty, he hoped to be set free. He was very calm and friendly in his communication, almost serene. He wrote some poetry, and he wanted to write a book about human emotions. Since only one inmate can have the same visitor on his visitors list, I could not come to see him, being Troy's visitor and feeling obliged to use the limited time of each visit with him. Therefore, the Puerto Rican and I began to exchange letters. I tried to give my Puerto Rican acquaintance—friend?—some encouragement and advice for using his time in prison in preparation for the real world and for writing the book about human emotions, and I sent him the collection of my own short stories.

The Puerto Rican answered with poetry and a report of the unbelievably confused situation of the family he was born into and grew up in. Everybody always drifted into crime and violence as a way of life. Should you be grateful if born into a decent family? He was just longing for peace and light and human harmony. I advised him to try to remove himself and stay away from that kind of environment. It would only lead him back to where he came from and put a final end to a free life. But how could he possibly follow this advice, not knowing any other world and not having any human anchors in any different environment? If he was not strong and did not find help, I predicted that loneliness and need would drive him back to his people and into more trouble.

Meanwhile, I had received all the documents from Troy relating to his trial ten years earlier about the murder of his wife. The documents did not look good for him, convincingly detailing, as they did, the accusations against him. But Troy's account was so different. Which side could you believe? Were the documents those false testimonies, or was Troy's vision of reality disturbed? "You know what I mean," the neighbors had said about him.

We spent every one of the many visits with him in prison over a year's time discussing his innocence and his attempt to have all judgments against him reversed in appeal.

Troy was treated well in prison. As the oldest inmate, he was allowed to use the library every day for his legal research. He was even allowed to start a small flower patch in one of the courtyards. I asked him whether he would not possibly be better off staying in prison, where he would be well taken care off, rather than living alone on welfare in that rough part of town.

"No," he said. He wanted the truth to come out, as a matter of principle and justice, and he wanted to walk out into the world with his head held up.

How could I not believe in Troy, the one I saw in front of me and talked to?

As time went by, I could not converse with Troy about anything but legal maneuvering—which rendered the visits increasingly less humanely valuable. Troy was understandably obsessed with his case and full of confidence that he would be released within a very short time.

I talked to friends about the case. Most of them were afraid that Troy would actually be free again—and possibly also that the Puerto Rican would be free. They told me that the typical pattern of such situations would be that Troy and the Puerto Rican would show up at my doorstep, asking for help and, not finding help anywhere else, expecting to be taken in by us. Worst of all, they might bring their buddies along or tell them of our home, attracting them there as well.

One night, rather late, I received a phone call. A rather strange voice addressed me with my full name, asking for support and referring to the Puerto Rican in jail. Had he not indicated that his brother was also in jail and the other siblings were in trouble with the law? Were they now coming after me?

Hearing this, our sons insisted that I cut off the prison contacts in order to protect Eva, their mother. My lawyer friend supported their view and indicated that Troy would, most likely, be set free before long.

I most sincerely hope that Troy will be found innocent. I wish that I could drive by Troy's house again, to stop and see his radiant face and wonderful smile, admire his beautiful flowers, and have a friendly chat with him. I wish that I could see my Puerto Rican friend set free, too, particularly if he could remove himself from his old environment, as I so strongly recommended to him. He could pursue his technical trade, possibly with a newfound wife, and write poetry on the side. I would like to drive with both of them to the seashore or to the mountains and breathe the fresh air in freedom. I would like to see them each build a fulfilled life, before it would be too late. Life is unique and so short.

If only the temper of both of them, Troy and the Puerto Rican, would keep them out of trouble and darkness, that neither they nor any innocent victims would get hurt any longer. How much damage is done by rage in the world? Will there ever be a dependable medical or psychological cure for bad temper, ire, and rage? Would it have helped if they had had better friends early in life?

What can we do? Restrain ourselves before lecturing others or before becoming their models for better or worse. Should we be better friends to our fellow human travelers through life, close or distant, before they or we, ourselves, get into trouble?

*

The courts rejected Troy's appeal.

The Phantom of the Internet

*

*A story for the experienced and addicted owner
of a personal Web site*

*

*This is a story that only owners of personal Web sites or their friends
and relatives should read and can appreciate. All other readers please
move on to another story. I don't want to scare you unnecessarily.*

*Web sites—they should be called Web buildings—can be
compared to real estate. Of course, they are virtual real estate.
They do not exist in the real world but exist only on virtual
ground, whatever that is. You can get small sites, comparable to
city apartments, for free from telephone companies or internet
connection providers. Compared to real apartments, they are not
wide and not deep; usually they contain only enough room for
some biographical information about the owner or, say, a report on
Aunt Jane's seventieth birthday.*

*Larger Web sites belong to sports clubs. They have one room
for listing upcoming events and another for showing the winners
of the last games. Sometimes these Web sites have a separate lobby,
the so-called welcome page or home page you see upon first typing
in the web address.*

*Professional Web sites are a cut above all that. They cost a
monthly fee of $14.95 and are spacious spaces, millions of bits wide
and deep, with beautiful architecture and an impressive sounding*

address. The bourgeois sites merely end with ".com," which is read as "dot com". The high-brow ones end with "dot edu" and are of an academic nature, even if reporting only the newest research on the life expectancy of some bug in the Amazon jungle.

The nobility among Web sites reside in the "dot orgs," belonging to real or make-believe organizations for the common good of mankind, who usually start by asking for donations. Beware! There are some lowly players, like in real life, who quickly start a little foundation in order to acquire a dot-org address, then collect donations and do not pay taxes ever after.

I am only a dot-com citizen and supposed to be proud of that.

As in real estate, you become attached to your own property as you grow into

the world of Web sites. You start timidly, small when young, and progress with age and success to more imposing property. The casual composition of a first poem or the writing of a first story suffices for some friends or relatives to urge you to "put it on the web."

How do you do that, and why? "There are people around who can teach you, you know. Just get one of those smart young kids who know everything about computers. Come on, be modern. How else can we read your writings in a proper way?"

It took a year of such talk to make me put an ad in the local university's student paper in search of a Web site architect—yes, that's what they are called. After all, they build something on your empty lot in cyberspace or modify what you may already have, like putting an addition on the back of your house. Even the famous architect Michael Graves once started by designing additions to private residences. He built one for our house at a time when ordinary people could still afford his services. Now, we can only afford to buy one of those tea kettles he designs.

Within days of placing the ad, I found a student to act as my Web site architect. He wanted $25 per hour. I was scared. Just calculate: twenty-five times a few hundred is a substantial sum. I contracted for a simple start, just trying to get my feet—or my toes—wet.

What happened? Within a few hours, the student had established a Web site with my first story already posted. He had done an outstanding job. The site looked great and even appeared in two different colors. My wife complimented me. I felt that I had to pay the student more than his bill. How could I avail myself of the support of such a sophisticated and friendly expert 'architect,' who had constructed a whole Web site, and not pay at least as much for his time as I would for a plumber's?

The next step soon followed. Didn't I want to know who was looking at my Web site? Certainly! The student set me up with some "traffic reports." A simple one is called "Tracker." In addition, there was the one provided by my internet connection provider for free, and, finally, there was a sophisticated one called the "Summary Report." Wow! I was impressed.

Within a very short time the traffic reports showed that I had a number of "hits," the term for counting the number of visits to my Web site by people in cyberspace. I could hardly believe it. Had I already become famous?

Only later did I learn that these visits were merely from search engines like Inktomi and Googlebot, which look at any and all Web sites, regardless of their worth or their standing in cyberspace, in order to be able to report what to find or what to expect on all the Web sites out there. These search engines may account for more than a hundred hits per day, or about 20 to 50 percent of all the hits coming to your Web site.

But I was hooked. I began to share my real life and love with my Web site. I kept writing more and more material to put on the site, and watched the traffic reports more and more often to see how my readership grew.

Exciting news! I had readers from other countries—Canada and Australia at first, then the UK, Germany, and more—soon from dozens of countries.

That was the moment when this story began—the story of the "Phantom of the Internet," a story in five scenes, which may soon be found on my Web site. Please come and visit my Web site so my traffic report can record more hits!

*

Scene One: Middle Age

A man named Ygor wrote stories about the country in which his ancestors once lived. They were stories of ordinary people, of heroes, and of ghosts. Ghosts, because Ygor had a dark streak, dreaming of the fantastic and letting his mind roam through vast spaces of his thoughts; some were light, some very dark.

Ygor also wrote about philosophy, and then he wrote about spirituality. He developed a theory of the origin and function for the whole world. He also wrote short stories. One Web site was not enough for all this material. Soon he had two! There are few people in cyberspace who need, and actually have, two Web sites. Not even the dot-orgs have that, normally.

Ygor actually had two.

Ygor wrote almost daily—much to the chagrin of his lovely wife. He developed a curved posture from constantly bending over the keyboard of his computer.

Scene Two: In Retirement

Thirty years went by. Thirty wonderful years—or what could have been wonderful years. Spring filled the garden with flowers. Summer let everybody go on vaca-tion—everybody? Winter was time to frolic in the snow, if you were not sitting inside behind the computer as Ygor did.

Ygor had become a computer addict—or, should I say, an internet addict.

In the morning, Ygor's first action was to look at the traffic reports for the previous day. Happy was the day when the reported count was over five hundred hits in one day. Miserable was the day when the count was down below four hundred. There once was a day with 750 hits, but there was another one with only 375.

When Ygor came down to breakfast, delayed by this report evaluation, his darling wife immediately knew where things stood. By then, she had finished her coffee and read the newspaper and was ready to move on. Ygor's thoughts were already on what he would write that day or how he could change his Web site to attract more hits.

How do you attract more hits from Web site visitors? For one, there were the titles of each essay. Each story required careful wording so certain search words would provide for high positioning within

Google's search lists. Then there were the hidden titles in the hidden code of each piece and its associated index code page, both accessible only by the little-known WordPad software. Again, suitable titles and words had to be found for that index page code.

Then, you can evaluate to see whether the changes in search words had made a difference in the number of visitors and their hits.

Mostly, they didn't, but sometimes they did, as you will see.

Scene Three: End of the Trail

By his later years, Ygor had learned the intricacies of improving reader response. On his Web site, little areas called out for his visitors to "Contact the author with your comments or questions." When a reader clicked on those links, a little form appeared, which the reader could fill out for the author and, with another click, send an e-mail to the owner of the Web site or whoever was programmed as the recipient of the form.

Ygor went far beyond this, however. He set up a memory base of his own, containing birthdays of all his friends and relatives, for example. He set up a "crawler" of his own, capable of finding the actual day of the week for each date of the year. When a birthday came along, a congratulatory e-mail addressed to the right name went out automatically.

He added other features. The memory base contained a bit of personal information about each relative and friend. Hence, the congratulatory notes would refer to that information—hobbies, collections, sports interests, for example. One such note read: "Congratulations, Joe, on your thirty-seventh birthday. I hope you will have a good day of golf today, and don't forget to drink your bottle of Miller Light beer afterwards!"

As the crawler capability expanded, the e-mails became more sophisticated— making reference to the daily weather in the area of the recipient of the mail and to events in his or her hobby realm.

Finally, the crawler pretty much knew as much as any person would know— or was able to find out on the web. The e-mails became indistinguishable from real letters you or I would write. The recipients could even reply—and most questions found counter-answers in a response. A friend's question of "How are you?" was easy for the automatic Web site to answer. The answers came in a random mix between "Just fine" and "Today is not such a good day for me—the weather, you know!"

Ygor established an endowment to provide automatic payment for his Web site and e-mail charges for many years into the future. Consequently, even after he died, the congratulatory notes kept going out to his relatives and friends— unless they had notified his Web site of their own demise.

The weird thing about this program was that Ygor's wife kept getting letters from him—just the way he used to write them and with actual reference to daily events—even though he was long dead. Eerie! Ghostly!

Scene Four: The Phantom Appears, or Does It?

Ygor's wife could take it no longer. She contacted the Web site hosting company and the internet connection company, asking for everything to be disconnected, in one bold stroke of cyber-euthanasia killing what was left of Ygor's spirit.

What Ygor's wife had not known, however, was that a friend of Ygor's—if you can call him a friend—had hijacked his Web site by simple hacking. Afraid that this new Ygor site would be cut off as soon as he had resurrected Ygor's spirit, the hacker programmed it to appear only at irregular intervals and from a wide selection of different internet servers at random.

Ygor had become a true phantom—the Phantom of the Internet!

Now, it could happen that a friend of Ygor's was happily tapping away at his computer and was suddenly interrupted with Ygor's image on his screen together with a friendly note relating to the events of the day, or worse. An instant later, it was gone, leaving no trace in the inbox or any memory location, only to appear again days, months, or years later.

Scene Five: The Final Bang.

Word about the "Phantom of the Internet" quickly got around. People wanted to participate in this phenomenon.

Then, it became possible to subscribe to the "Phantom," to be put on the mail list of recipients—that way you could expect phantom appearances.

So far, so good. But then, a presidential election approached. The phantom took a strident approach to politics. Finally, "he" (after all, the phantom was Ygor's spirit) requested that his readers write him in when voting. The phantom was elected with a clear majority as the next president of the country.

Actually, many politicians are not much more than phantoms of the advisors who direct them and provide them with media presence—even some famous women politicians can and do appear that way.

The phantom began his term as president by hiring Karl Rove as consultant and handler of the phantom appearances—a very clever and successful move, providing all the ideas for the phantom's later statements and actions. Next, he presented his cabinet and political program and pushed it forcefully day by day.

By now, the previously short images of Ygor on the computers had become video clips showing him speaking—with a synthetic voice modeled after that of a famous actor who had been president some years before.

Until a gigantic power failure hit the whole country. It started with a small rodent biting through the insulation of a control cable of the power grid somewhere in the Midwest, but the whole country went dark.

The video images and the voice of the phantom ceased to rule.

The entire country began to experience a spiritual vacuum.

But the phantom's wife finally found peace.

Moral

How can we protect ourselves against this sort of thing ever happening?

Let's throw away all our computers.

Let's go back to mechanical typing machines and use the normal postal services to transport our letters.

Let's stop listening to synthetic political voices without the real depth of life.

Let's embrace our lovely wives and leave more time for their wonderful company while we are still together in this beautiful world.

*

If Ygor were still alive, he would now turn off his computer and look for a new hobby.

And you?

Fortune Comes, Fortune Goes

*Hear, hear: perceive opportunity, grasp opportunity,
and don't misjudge opportunity*

*

*Why do so many people stagnate in their lives while others, at
the same time and from similar backgrounds, find their fortune?
Is it their fault that fortune passes them by, that there are no
opportunities in their lives? Are the others just "in the right place
at the right time," as the saying goes? Or has it something to do
with perceiving and grasping opportunity when it shows itself?
The following is written as an informative story for youngsters,
almost as a lecture. But it could also be useful for those who
struggle or stagnate in their later lives and is based on some years
of experience.*

*

Joe, still a young man, spent much of his free time sitting on a bench
in the town park and dreaming in a mood of utter melancholy. Life
was miserable, life was boring, and there was no way out. Was that all
there was to life? Was it worth continuing like that? Joe had been the
employee of a large company and had done the same work—over and
over—for years. He was so bored and disappointed with life that he
did not do good work, and finally, he was let go. He was a little afraid.

How could his life continue, how could he support himself in dignity, how could he ever afford to have a family of his own?

As he was sitting in the park one sunny morning, just staring at the ground in front of him, he did not notice a wonderful appearance floating by. She looked like one of the goddesses Botticelli or another of the Italian Renaissance artists could have painted—half angel, half goddess, and almost transparent in her beauty. This was Fortuna, the goddess of good luck.

She looked at Joe and smiled. Then she waved at him with a small bouquet of flowers as if telling him to follow her.

Joe did not notice her, and she floated by, down through the park, until another person noticed her and followed her, to be led to the secret gate of happiness.

A friend of Joe's observed the scene from a distance. He went over to Joe and asked him why he hadn't followed Fortuna.

"Oh, I just didn't see her," came the answer.

"How could this happen to you?" admonished his friend, or was it Joe's father? "You must keep your eyes open!"

Several weeks later, after autumn had come, Joe was sitting there again. Nothing had changed in his life. He was as discouraged as ever. But now, he was looking forward and to the right and left, just in case Fortuna came by again.

Little did Joe notice that Fortuna floated by behind the bench he was sitting on, where he could not see her without turning completely around. She even stopped for a moment and waved again with her beautiful flowers, inviting Joe to follow her. But he hadn't looked around, only forward and right and left. Once again, he did not follow her. And, again, someone else in the park was the lucky one. Later, the newspapers wrote about the big invention that person had announced on that day, how he had started a company with that idea and was on his way to a fulfilled life.

The same friend had observed this second scene with Fortuna. This time, he became almost angry at Joe.

"You cannot just search for Fortuna where you choose. You must look all around, especially where you've never looked before. And when you see her—if you ever do again—you must grab her and hold on. Don't let her disappear again. Hold on to her. Next time, make her lead you to the secret gate of happiness."

Joe was crushed. He had missed another big chance.

Some time later, he was again sitting on his accustomed park bench. Winter had started, and life had become particularly bleak for Joe. Fortuna, however, showed compassion. For yet a third time, she came by and approached him—this time from the side. She even stopped and tapped him on the shoulder. Joe was electrified. He quickly turned around and, almost instinctively, grasped her so she could not disappear again. Gently she led him until they came to the gate of happiness. She opened it and showed him a part of the park he had never perceived before. There, high on a hill stood a beautiful building.

"This will be yours, if you walk up the hill," Fortuna said.

Joe did not let his chance go by. He walked up the hill, even though he had to struggle. It took him much longer than he had thought it would. He had all the perseverance to deserve the prize. Finally, he had found his approach to a fulfilled life.

Is this the end of the story? Not quite yet!

The devil had also seen what was going on and how Fortuna selected some lucky winners. He thought to himself, "I can do that, too, and gain my own benefit from that."

Next day, the devil dressed up like Fortuna. The beautiful veil didn't quite fit over his horns, and the wide skirt didn't quite hide his big claw foot. But there he went.

Sure enough, he saw someone sitting on a park bench and dreaming, actually looking quite happy and well situated in life. This was just the right person for the devil. He danced back and forth before that person, showing off some beautiful jewel-decorated boxes.

That person who observed the devil was a bit naïve and, furthermore, overly greedy. Without investigating any further what kind of fellow the devil was and whether those boxes were decorated with real jewels or just fakes, he (or was it a "she"?) grasped for the boxes. The devil did not let go and guided that person to the gate of disappointment. Once there, he pushed the person into his own dismay while the jeweled boxes dissolved into thin air. The devil made the poor fellow surrender all his possessions before he let him go as a ruined man.

*

What do you make of this?

You may be a student in a big college and not know what profession to pursue in life—or you may be an employee in a big company and not know whether you will ever have a chance to move up.

Years later, you may read that some students at the same university came up with a brilliant idea, started a company, and became very successful. Or you may hear that somebody from the same division of the company had a brilliant business idea, was promoted, and became the president or changed employment and prospered thereafter or changed from being an engineer and, after a couple of years of demanding evening studies, became a successful patent lawyer.

Why did these things happen for them and not for you?

Very few lives ever pass totally without opportunity. You have to look around for opportunities. You have to perceive opportunities; you have to show initiative in grasping an opportunity; and you have to develop perseverance in pursuing an opportunity. Then you will succeed.

Sometimes several opportunities may be open to you at once, and you have to choose. That may be difficult, but whatever you choose, if suitable and if pursued with perseverance, may lead to a fulfilled life. Just go ahead, and don't just sit there.

However—there is this big however—you must avoid the false opportunities, the temptations presented by the devil, the opportunities you don't know anything about, and the get-rich-quick stock tips from strangers. You must be knowledgeable. You must show judgment, and not fall for the temptations that will take all you have away from you and leave you ruined. That, too, has happened to many others before you.

Now, get up, learn something useful about the area in which you are interested, and develop your judgment; hone it. Then look for the opportunity, grasp it with initiative, courage, and determination, and persevere until Fortuna fulfills her promise.

If, however, you find out that you have fallen for the devil, know how to get out and start over once more with another and better opportunity. Fortuna is still around and ready if you are.

The Very Short Life of a Tiny Fly

*

*She lived for only one day, but that one so fully that
just one additional day to live would have been her greatest happiness!*
*

*Why are we sometimes in a mood of seeing our lives as dull and
of little value and of not expecting much joy in our lives anymore?
We withdraw from everything, as if ready to pass away at any
moment, or we ponder all we have already lost in life or will soon
lose. At other times, our life may pass in an internal emptiness
or dullness. Nothing seems to have meaning or significance for us
when we are in those moods—the most superficial entertainments
or routines fill our days. Why do we abandon the fullness that our
life could still have? Fulfill every day! Life can be so wonderful,
even if only for a few moments here and there.*

*When I walk through our garden in summer, I sometimes
encounter some tiny flies, often dancing around in the sun in a
dynamic whirl. A zoologist friend told me that they live for only
one day. This is the story that occurred to me when I heard that.*

*

A wonderful summer morning dawned. From under a great apple tree
behind a farmhouse, out of abandoned fruit from last year, arose a tiny
fruit fly. It stretched its new wings and flew up to a high branch of the

tree. For the first time, this tiny fly observed the brilliance and beauty of a sunny morning. What a wonder it was to be alive!

There were many leaves on the tree all around the little fly. Have you ever stopped to marvel at a small group of leaves on a large tree? Did you ever consider breaking off just one of those small twigs with only a few leaves on it? Did you ever put such a twig in a vase and marvel at it, as at a work of great art? You could paint a picture of this twig or take a photograph of it. Such a picture might be selected for a prize. But think about it! That tree was full of such twigs—thou-sands of small bunches of artistically arranged leaves—and you had never before noticed them. How wonderful is our world, if only we have eyes for it and take time to look out for its wonders. It takes just a little moment of our time, which we sometimes have too much of, just a little of the time that is still left for us in this world, just a small part of this day, to possibly let it become a truly fulfilled day in our lives.

The sun began to shine brightly, and the air felt warm. The little fly flew over to the yard behind the farmhouse. How nice it was to be able to move around from one place to an entirely different one, just as you want—to always see something new and find new experiences. Did you ever intensely enjoy moving around, even just to another room, to walk just once around the block, to drive just for a quarter of an hour to nowhere, or to travel?

The little fly noticed that some clouds had appeared in the sky. Some of them looked like little round pillows. In between, there were some stretched clouds that looked as if they had been placed there by a swift stroke of a brush. Who had painted them so nicely? The clouds changed appearance as time went by. How many clouds may have sailed away over your head during your lifetime? And how many of those did you actually perceive and enjoy? An old lady lived all alone, but she had a harmonic inner disposition. She told everybody that she observed the clouds all day long, every day. That was an ever new experience for her, the dramatic change and art of nature, and that alone let her enjoy her life.

The tiny fly observed all the agricultural equipment in back of the farmhouse. What a different world that was! Every detail of those machines had been designed with great intelligence to serve the farmer in support of his family in an often difficult world. Those machines and their supporting industry permit all of us to live more or less comfortably.

How interesting would it be to understand just a little more of the mental content of all technology or, more so, of the sciences, which help us actually comprehend nature and the whole universe we live in. After all, be aware that we exist in an intellectually understandable world. Don't always read only the newspaper and entertaining novels! Take some time to understand the sciences, to understand the world on which we have the great opportunity to live for a while, even if this requires more effort.

The morning had almost passed and the time came for our tiny fly to join its peer group. After all, we don't live alone in this world. But we must show initiative to join and be received by others. That's why our little fly rose up and soon encountered a whole swarm of its own kind over a small bush in the farmer's garden. There, the flies flew around, by the hundreds or by the thousands, in many circles, forming a wildly circulating column—so many tiny specks of light in the brightness of the summer sun.

Their dance got ever wilder and became an exciting experience for our fly—to meet so many others, to be part of that group. Was this the meaning of life: to be dedicated to the group, to the community? Nature compensates us for our commitment to others with emotions of warmth and joy. How mysterious are all those emotions that give value to our lives.

A swallow swooped right into the middle of the swarm. Afterwards, some of the little flies were missing. Did the swallow just gulp them down? How dark this world could be. One of the tiny flies had a wing torn off! Our little fly flew down to it and recognized one of her sisters from waking that morning under the old fruit tree. She remained for a long time to comfort her. She even brought her a droplet of water. Was helping the deepest purpose of living in a swarm? Was it this help that provided the deepest fulfillment?

But then she was drawn back to her partners, especially one whom she had met just before in the swarm. She experienced that very special happiness of being united with a partner in life. If she had not returned to the swarm, she could not have found him. Had she looked for the perfect and ideal partner, she could not have found him. But if both were ready to accept the other as they were, then, as long as they both were striving toward the light, they could rise together.

By now, it had turned late afternoon. The sun began to sink in the sky. At this time, it became important to care for offspring, for those that should emerge next year. She had to find and prepare a good place for them. Our little fly searched for quite some time to find the ideal place for all her little eggs where there was not too much competition from the others yet. She needed a place that would protect her offspring from the scavenging birds, but where the rays of the sun would still reach and where there was enough food for their first phase in life as larvae. What don't all parents do for their offspring and, in doing so, find their own happiness, even knowing that, most likely, they will not participate in their offspring's happiness later on!

Evening arrived. Our tiny fly became tired. Flying around was no longer easy. All the other flies had retreated into their hideaways, one by one. Should she just sit and complain? No, she flew once more into the farmer's garden to the nicest bush she had ever seen. Then she flew back up to the fruit tree from whence she had come and sat down on a high branch under a protecting leaf.

From there, she looked out onto the great, wide world. But, as time went by, it was less and less the view of the large world that gave her joy, especially since it was becoming less visible in the increasing darkness. But close by, there was still much beauty to see until her horizon contracted and she could now perceive only the wonderful group of leaves closest to her.

Finally, total darkness arrived. The eyes of our tiny fly closed.

What a wonderful and fulfilled day this was, she thought as she fell asleep. Oh, if I could have just one more day of life like this one. How I would try to fulfill that one too!

*

I wish for a wonderful day tomorrow for you and me. And, after that, I wish us many more—seven days in every week that may be given to you or me, 365 days in only one year.

But next time you walk through a garden and happen to see one of those tiny flies, salute her with a smile and leave her in peace as she pursues the business of her short life. Wish for a fulfilled day—for her and for yourself.

Guiding Lights in My Life

*

*Thanks to the exceptional individuals who gave
light and direction to my early life*

*

*When thinking about my early life, from childhood through
adolescence and on to an established existence, certain moments
of light come to my mind. Those were moments when the
world suddenly appeared better, when new perspectives or new
opportunities for a more fulfilled life opened up. Those moments
were always related to some person who projected a new emotion or
a new mental direction into my life that allowed me to go forward.
I am deeply grateful to those individuals and would like to leave
this story as a small memento for them.*

*

My parents, my light and guides in early childhood:

I gratefully remember the contribution my parents made to the light
and strength of my life. My father had a strong personality and a
wide mental horizon. He allowed me to participate in increasingly
challenging activities and showed me the beauty of nature. Many
conversations with him contributed to the development of my mind.
His support gave me strength.

My mother, the heart of the family with her warm emotions, had an always positive spirit in her contact with or judgment of others and in coping with life in general.

I should write much more about both of my parents, but I consider my family a private matter, and I would like to ask the reader for understanding while I continue writing about other, nonrelated individuals of positive significance in my early life.

Mr. Behr, the teacher of my first class in grade school:

At the end of a wonderful summer in Berlin, at age six, the day came for me to go to school. As was typical in those days, I carried a backpack with a slate board, a chalk pencil, and a small sponge attached to a long string—all to use for writing, drawing, and correcting. We were directed to a classroom where a tall, thin, and energetic teacher waited for us. He bade us sit behind the standard school desks of that time and demanded absolute quiet and silence. Then he talked for a while.

The boy next to me, who had been fiddling with his slate board, suddenly dropped it with a loud clatter, and the whole class laughed. The teacher came over holding a slender bamboo cane in his hand and touched the boy's fingers, telling him to sit quietly. In my mind, the teacher had hit the boy, and I was shocked by this expression of violence. The next day, a short distance from home on the way to school, I could not walk any further. I stood there, frozen by fear, until neighbors called my parents to come and take me home.

Within a few days, I was enrolled in a different school. The teacher there, Mr. Behr, was a bit older and had a somewhat rotund figure. As we arrived in the morning, he took a violin out of an old case that was lined with blue velvet and played some wonderful music. Then, he had several of us tell him what we had done the day before and what we wanted to learn, while he listened attentively.

Later during the school year, whenever one of us had a birthday, Mr. Behr would bring a small cake and candle and would play a special tune just for that happy child. No question: we all adored Mr. Behr and did everything we could to please him. The strange world away from home became beautiful. Learning became a delight. We began to move out into our own lives.

Thank you, Mr. Behr, for saving me and for opening a joyful path for my life!

A boy named von Zastrow and the "Waldstein Sonata":

When in my early teens, I found myself in a boarding school in Davos, high in the Alps of Switzerland, at that time the European center of sanatoriums for lung diseases. For the first time, I was separated from my family and all my former friends. It was at that age that I began to experience desolate loneliness, which became a theme of my life.

There were youngsters with tuberculosis or severe asthma. But there were also some bullies and some wild ones. Only one in our class appeared to be a wimp. He was always friendly, but he did not participate in any group activities. His only interest was in playing the piano.

In the evening, after finishing my homework, I would go to bed early, so as to be in the dark by myself, in loneliness and sadness. The window of my room opened onto the schoolyard. On the other side of the yard was the classroom building that contained a music room. That was where Zastrow went quite often to practice the piano in the evening. I must confess that I had refused to learn the piano while still at home and had rather cut classes at that time so that I could go sailing on a small boat on the lake. Now at boarding school, Zastrow's music— the endless finger exercises, *études*, or the wild music of a strange composer—dis-turbed me.

The deep darkness and loneliness of a particular night in winter was especially hard on me. My thoughts were interrupted by the beginning of Zastrow's music. It started wild, as always. But this time, in the second movement of his playing, the *adagio* harmonies felt somewhat warmer to me, yet still quite dark. Then, all of a sudden, a wonderful melody with tender sounds wove into the course of that sonata.

Immediately I felt wide-awake. Moments later, the melody returned—a bit clearer, lighter, and more forthright than before. My heart began to feel joy. As that melody returned again and again, I had found a new light in life. Life could be beautiful and worth living.

After the music had ended, I fell asleep and enjoyed a wonderful night of internal harmony. The next day I talked to von Zastrow. He told me that he had played Beethoven's "Waldstein Sonata," the piece he liked most. We talked for a while, and I found that he was just a youngster like me, but with greater sensitivity. Music was his way of coping with life—and now it had become a source of light in life for me.

Thank you, von Zastrow, for showing me a path out of the darkness within me.

Mr. Gerber, a high school teacher of Greek:

Mr. Gerber was a somewhat older, Swiss teacher of small stature and always very correct behavior. He could have been a bureaucrat, but instead he was our teacher of classical Greek in my junior year of high school. Endless were the lectures and hours of homework dedicated to irregular verbs and the difficult grammar of that ancient language. Boring were the hours of line-by-line translation of classical texts, proceeding in small sections.

Then came the news of the end of World War II. The carnage had stopped, but what was left? At that age, we had little understanding of the new situation and what it meant for us, since we had been living securely in Switzerland. However, Mr. Gerber, who had a wider view of history, knew. He must have seen that the true winners of that war were the United States and Russia. Germany had come to its moral and physical end. France's cultural leadership of Europe had yielded to that of America. England's mercantile and colonial empire was beginning to crumble. The other countries of Europe had become marginalized. Europe as we had known it had come to an end. Would its spirit survive in the West? Could something new arise from the ashes?

One morning, Mr. Gerber came to class as usual. We sat there with our grammar books and *Selected Reading* texts open, ready to go to work. He told us to close all those books. He had decided to tell us what the importance of the Greek spirit and of classical Europe had been.

Over the next hour, Mr. Gerber presented a fantastic world to us, one that we never had envisioned behind those rules of grammar and tedious translations. He spoke to us about the birth of our culture, about the opening of the human spirit to mental inquiry and clarity, and about the meaning of freedom in democracies based on law, the beginning of our Europe. He read a beautifully translated passage from the Odyssey, then the famous Pericles speech about the great spirit of Athens, and, finally, from some Greek philosophers.

As he spoke, he grew from his modest appearance to appear a great spirit and educator himself.

When the hour was over, applause arose from our class, something I had never heard in high school before.

Mr. Gerber walked silently out of the room, soon to end his modest career in retirement.

That day, our minds grew beyond the level of high school. That day we began to realize that a higher path was asked from our lives.

Thank you, Mr. Gerber, for letting us see what Europe and the West meant and what our task and opportunity would be to pursue!

Dr. Ludwig Lippmann, my mentor in difficult years:

Dr. Ludwig Lippmann grew up in Berlin and served as an aerial photographer in World War I, taking pictures of the front lines from small planes with open cockpits and without parachutes. Later, he became a well-known chemist. Dr. Lippmann, member of a highly regarded Jewish family, emigrated from Berlin to Ascona, Switzerland, at the last moment before the Nazis began the annihilation of the Jews. My father, Dr. Lippmann's best friend, helped him to safety and to transfer his financial resources.

When my family could no longer support me in boarding school, I ended up in a Swiss camp with many other foreign youngsters in trouble after the war. As soon as Dr. Lippmann, by then in his sixties and living in modest circumstances, heard that I was in a camp without a school, he took action. Within a short time, he relocated me to a refugee children's home in Ascona, where a chance to finish high school appeared likely. For the next few years, Dr. Lippmann—"Uncle Ludwig," as I had called him from childhood on—became my mentor.

We met about once a week for dinner. The meals were simple; the conversations were the essence of our meetings. The topics ranged widely from the sciences to politics, the arts, philosophy, and human nature. Dr. Lippmann had remained a German patriot—I should say he had remained an admirer of and continued to identify himself with classical German culture, of the times of Goethe, Schiller, the Humboldts, and other great philosophers and scientists. He hoped that the nightmare of the previous twelve years could be overcome and a new culture and spirit could arise again in Germany and in all of Europe. But what new culture was it that he was striving for? What could it be in our now changed and more modern time? That was the subject of many of our discussions.

In the end, the experience and learning from these discussions was not a solution to our mental question. Rather, I became acquainted with, and was guided by, a highly admirable old-line European individual's coping with modern life. Dr. Lippmann's intellectual rationality was superior—not only in his knowledge, but in his surprising mental associations, abstractions, and discovery of new perspectives. Equally important, his intellect was combined with a deep humanitarian empathy of the heart and a sense of personal responsibility. Then, too, there was his very fine and often complex humor. He gave short answers that could dissolve complex arguments in laughter, or he made impromptu observations that brought all haughtiness back to Earth or that were just plain funny. His humor was a reminder of the famous popular humor once found in old Berlin. A mental sovereignty resulted from this combination and gave him the resilience and strength to cope with his difficult life in a confusing world. Wasn't that wisdom?

Thank you, Uncle Ludwig, for guiding me into a life of a questioning rationality, warm human empathy, personal responsibility, and a little humor.

Lilly Volkart, who founded and managed a home for troubled children:

Where could I have lived without any financial resources while hoping to attend high school in Ascona? Only at Lilly Volkart's Home for Children on the "Collina," the hill above the town. Lilly had founded the home to help children in trouble after very difficult years in her own younger life. The famous Pestalozzi had brought Switzerland a tradition of new approaches to education. Lilly may have exceeded him.

"My children," as she called those referred to her by social workers in the larger or industrial cities of Switzerland, found harmony, self-esteem, and blossomed again. By the end of Nazi persecution of Jews in World War II, Lilly had accepted almost one hundred Jewish children in her home—all of whom had miraculously been transferred by their parents to Switzerland. Then Lilly accepted me, too, and leveraged her influence in that small town to have the local Benedictine monastery school admit me to its graduating class for that year. I am grateful to both Lilly and the Benedictines.

During the time that I stayed at Lilly's Home, I worked endless hours to catch up with a new language (Italian) and a new curriculum, and then, there were also the chores for the Home that were expected of each child. The highlight of each day was the late evening conversation with Lilly. The older children and I surrounded her in her combination living room, dining room, and office. Talk flowed freely, from the various daily experiences of the children to questions about the Home to unique characters of the small town to the life of the community in general to stories from the past.

In the most natural way possible, Lilly let every one of the children talk about his or her life and, in so talking, develop his or her thoughts, perspectives, and goals—or report about his or her problems and probe for solutions. When talking about other people, she never allowed us to "tear them apart." Talking about them was always a way of understanding them, while not necessarily condoning their attitudes.

Lilly had a penchant for spirituality, for seeing more in life than biology, psychology, and getting ahead. Was there not something higher in existence? Something that we did not yet understand, but that might be more meaningful?

What mainly counted for Lilly was what a person did in life that was good.

Wasn't that also wisdom?

Thank you, Lilly, for giving to my young life some warmth, a search for deeper meaning, the attempt to understand others before criticizing them, and the always humble striving for doing good.

Dr. George Sichling, a very creative mind:

My first job after college was in a small laboratory of a large company. My task was to incorporate the newly developed transistors into the then rapidly advancing field of robotics and automation. The fantasies of the media predicted that, in the not too distant future, robots would run all factories and humans would lead lives of leisure. But in our laboratory, we had to struggle with the problems of reality, and there, creativity counted.

Dr. Sichling was my supervisor in those days. It turned out that he had the most creative mind I've ever met. There were a few unusual approaches in his creative thinking. For example, he said that when you are faced with a new problem, you shouldn't go right away and read how other people have approached the problem or what existing solutions there are. First think about the problem yourself and write down your own ideas. Only then should you do an in-depth study of what other people thought. A newcomer often brings new perspectives to a problem and, hence, comes up with new ways to solve it.

The same applies when you are about to read a book about a new area of interest. First, think about that area and write down your own ideas. As before, you may have a new perspective that has been facilitated by your own experience and that could be different from what you are going to read. These ideas would become lost if you start by reading the thoughts of others.

Dr. Sichling always questioned the singular validity of any idea. He always looked for ways to find other, better, solutions. He greatly enjoyed getting involved in new fields of knowledge or study. In the course of his long life, he read about and discussed so many questions that, whenever something new came up, he found some interesting reference to completely different ideas or concepts, often resulting in very interesting creativity.

During my three years of working for Dr. Sichling, I accumulated quite a number of patent applications (all belonging to my employer). This led to my moving to California to become active in the field of aerospace electronics—the newest field of technical development and part of the wave that described innovation as the essence of America's future. A few years later, it led to the start of my own enterprise in this field of innovation. This was the culmination of a long-held dream.

Thank you, Dr. Sichling, for opening my mind to creativity and to new ideas.

Dr. Winkler, an energetic industrial entrepreneur of high standards:

Dr. Winkler's father started in the late 1800s as a door-to-door salesman of notions and ended as a significant textile manufacturer with factories in various parts of Germany. All of it crumbled in World War II. By then, his son, the young Dr. Winkler, had inherited one small spinning and weaving factory located on the Rhine, just north of the Swiss border. Within a few months after the end of the war, he had shirts—a precious commodity in those days—manu-factured there. He could barter the shirts for more cotton from the French occupation forces. He also bartered for food for his employees.

As soon as Germany stabilized after the war, and its currency regained some value, Dr. Winkler began a long-term cooperation with the most advanced Swiss textile machine manufacturer for the development of ever more advanced machines providing increased productivity while retaining flexibility. Fashions had to be followed and costs had to be lowered. That was the name of the game in textiles. Dr. Winkler built his business on excellence in performance and on trust—with a keen sense for business results.

After shirts, the production of handkerchiefs followed. The handkerchiefs featured colorful borders. Soon, everybody bought Winkler handkerchiefs. Later came the production of suits "on demand" that were delivered within two days from order. The "on demand" feature allowed for the reduction of inventories for department stores.

Winkler worked very hard and was always fully alert, focused, creative, economical, and driven to a degree that I had not seen in any other entrepreneur. When he was not working, he collected art and enjoyed the company of interesting people.

I had known Dr. Winkler for six years, and he always encouraged me to realize my goal of starting my own enterprise. When I was ready to start my business in aerospace electronics in California in 1959, Dr. Winkler financed the start-up, in exchange for a substantial part of the shares, of course.

Running a business was new to me. I made mistakes and had to learn. To succeed, I had to persevere, be inventive, and overcome problems with the help of excellent associates and employees. Winkler remained a role model of mine in striving for excellence and in conducting business based on trust, always fully alert, focused, creative, economical, and driven.

Thank you for your support in realizing my goals, Dr. Winkler, and for remaining a role model when my early years came to an end and many years of life in industry followed.

∗ ∗ ∗ ∗

Was life always a sequence of positive steps for me? Were there also individuals with a negative impact on my life? Certainly. More than I would have wished.

I had to learn to cope with them. I preferred to evade them, but occasionally I had to fight them. The reality of life demands the Darwinian prevailing. Our culture (and the example of my father in a naval encounter in 1915 at sea) offers decent and, I hope, humane ways of doing so.

Were there additional positive individuals also later in my life? Certainly. I am deeply grateful to many of those. The joy, fulfillment, or meaning of life often came from contact with such positive individuals.

Most of them are still alive, or their direct relatives are. Please understand, dear reader, that I refrain from writing about contact with friends who are still present in my life.

After writing about the positive individuals in my life, could it be my turn now to pass on some light or support to somebody in the next generation?

∗ ∗ ∗ ∗

And now, at the end of all the short stories from my "Journey through Life," let me express special thanks to Eva, my travel companion through so many fulfilling years.

In you, as in a golden mirror, I often found reflected my thoughts and the stories as they came to my mind, with all their colorful characters, letting them appear more beautiful and more humane.

About the Author

For Helmut Schwab, the value of life comes from the warmth of human bonds, whether in the family, among friends, or in chance encounters. His experiences of the world with a human touch—in empathy, joy, or humor, but also in sympathy, sorrow, and suffering—inspired his short stories.

He found joy of life in observing the variety and beauty in nature, whether in grandiose scenery or minute detail and through his participation in various forms of the arts.

His academic training was in the sciences. He has worked in the aerospace and electronics industries. Most of his personal effort and writing concentrated on a deeper understanding of the universe, the biological world we live in, the human mind, and societies or cultures. Specifically, he concentrated on understanding the important human characteristics of mental creativity, ethical values, individual personality, and sensitivity for aesthetics and art.

Of greater personal importance to Helmut Schwab were questions of philosophy and theology, the phenomenon of religion, the dichotomy between science and religion, the question of the remaining transcendental foundation of our existence and the consequent meaning or purpose of our lives.

He has also pursued historical studies and studied the present conflict between the Muslim world and the West.

The essays resulting from all of these efforts can be found on the Web site "www.schwab-writings.com."

Schwab volunteered in the community, working for environmental issues and to improve conditions for the handicapped and for low-income families in our inner cities.

Appendix: Additional Writings
by
Helmut Schwab

The following essays can be found on the Web site www.schwab-writings.com and can be downloaded from there. The publication of some of these essays is in preparation.

Web site section "Science and Evolution"

Read the full essay by going to "Evolution: Understanding Physical and Mental Existence." But, for easier reading, that essay is also available in the following eight separate subsections:

1. Cosmogony, Cosmic Evolution, Evolution of Earth
2. Origin of Life, Molecular Biology, Natural Evolution, Humans
3. The Origin, Evolution and Functions of the Human Mind
4. The Origin, Evolution and Functions of Societies and Cultures
5. "Intelligent Design Theory" as Opposed to Natural Evolution
6. Extraterrestrial Intelligence? What Could It Mean to Us?
7. The Future and Expected End of Mankind and the Universe
8. Closing Comments and Conclusions

Web site section "Brain and Mind"

How mental creativity, ethical behavior, personality, sensitivity for aesthetics or art, and battle fatigue are anchored in neurophysiology, biochemistry, psychology, and one's own thought.

This section includes seven individual essays:
1. The Brain, the Mind: Creative Thought
2. The Brain, the Mind: Mental Creativity
3. The Brain, the Mind: Ethics, Overview
4. The Brain, the Mind, and Ethics
5. The Brain, the Mind: Human Personality
6. Aesthetics, Art, Culture
7. Brain, Mind: Battle Fatigue, PTSD, Combat Stress

Web site section "Philosophy and Theology: Meaning of Life and Truth in Religion, Science, Philosophy, Theology"

Addressing the basic questions of human existence—meaning, purpose, peace of soul, and strength to act—and the search for truth in religion.

This section includes the following five essays:
1. Meaning, Purpose, and Direction in Life
2. Astrophysics and Theology (also available in German)
3. Religion, What Is It, What Should It Be
4. Intelligent Design Theory vs. Evolution
5. Intelligent Design Theory: A Critical Analysis

Web site section "History and Politics"

This section includes two essays on history based on newly found source material:
1. A Biography of the Great Henry Villard
2. An Essay on the Paris Peace Conference of 1919

This section also includes two essays on special topics related to history or politics:

1. Islam, the Muslim World and the West.
2. The Spontaneous Historic Origin and Evolution of Cultures and Civilizations on Earth, Example Peru and Ecuador

Printed in the United States
131254LV00002B/346/P

9 780595 483457